Deathmark

Also by Kim Antieau

Novels
*The Blue Tail • Broken Moon • Butch
Church of the Old Mermaids • Coyote Cowgirl
The Desert Siren • The Fish Wife • Her Frozen Wild
The Gaia Websters • Jewelweed Station
The Jigsaw Woman • Maternal Instincts • Mercy, Unbound
Queendom: Feast of the Saints • The Rift • Ruby's Imagine
Swans in Winter • Whackadoodle Times
Whackadoodle Times Two*

Nonfiction
*Answering the Creative Call
Certified: Learning to Repair Myself and the World
in the Emerald City
Counting on Wildflowers: An Entanglement
Old Mermaids Book of Days and Nights
The Old Mermaids Oracle
The Salmon Mysteries:
a Reimagining of the Eleusinian Mysteries
The Salmon Mysteries Workbook:
Reimagining the Eleusinian Mysteries
Under the Tucson Moon*

Collections
*Entangled Realities (with Mario Milosevic)
The First Book of Old Mermaids Tales
Tales Fabulous and Fairy • Trudging to Eden*

Chapbook
Blossoms

Blog
www.kimantieau.com

Photography
www.kimantieau.smugmug.com

Deathmark

Kim Antieau

Green Snake
PUBLISHING

For Mario

One

If you think the world is a good and decent place, you haven't been paying attention. Either that or you're a moron.

And I'd know. About the world I mean. I've seen a lot of it. At least those cities served by that greying hound of hell called the bus line. Onward and downward. Mom usually in the seat next to me, snoring, sleeping off a drunk or the 'mares. Always on the lookout for a place to settle, to call home.

We'd been doing this for my whole sixteen years as far as I could remember. Me and Mom. We hardly ever stayed in a place for longer than a few months. Once we got settled, the Shadow Woman always showed up and then we went on the run again.

One year I got to stay in the same school for almost nine months. Ann Arbor, I think. They've got a university, right? And a Natural History Museum. I spent hours inside that museum, mostly staring at the skeleton of a T. Rex, wondering what it would be like to be that big, to be able to kick ass. I was a kid then. Ten maybe.

This last time, we were in Phoenix for six months. At least I want you to think it was Phoenix. Let's get this straight right from the outset. I'm changing the names, places, and facts about everything. Well, almost everything. The truth as I know it will remain the same. So we were in Phoenix. We lived in this huge house that looked like it was out in the desert but it was right in the city. It had a long driveway with cacti and desert-looking shrubs on either side it. The driveway was brick. Melissa swore that one day when her parents weren't home she was going to paint the driveway yellow. The house was so big I kept getting lost in it when we first moved in.

Melissa's parents owned the house. Mom and I lived in the back in the maid's quarters— because that's what my mom was. Their maid. Or housekeeper. What's the difference anyway? She cleaned up after them, answered the door, and sometimes cooked for them. It was a full-time job, believe you me. I don't know how these three people—yep, three people in that big old house— ever got along before they hired my mom. I helped out, too. When they weren't around, I folded the laundry, vacuumed, stuff like that.

I was never sure how Mom scored that gig, but it was one of the best places we had ever lived. No dregs of society. No great unwashed, as my mom liked to call our compatriot travelers. Just rich people with their measly problems. Plenty of food. A clean house. And Melissa.

The daughter Melissa. Every once in a while we went up to her room and hung out. I liked being in her room. She was nice, but she was a little too cheerful—or something. Like she had never had a bad day in her life. I think taking me up to her room was the worst thing she had ever done. Maybe she was nasty at school. I didn't know since she went to a private school. I went up to her room because I liked her smell. I liked the smell of her room. Kind of flowery and sweaty. It smelled like home. Like how I imagined home should smell. A real home.

But none of this has even the tinge of importance on it. Because we don't live in the big fancy house with the big fancy dumb rich people any more. Not that I think all rich people are dumb, but sometimes they don't seem all there, you know what I mean? Same with street people. A lot of them aren't all there either. The rich and the street should get together and have a party. Wouldn't that be something to see? A gathering of zombies, some better dressed than others.

I won't tell you which I thought was the better dressed, the rich or the street. Or which had their own personal style. After moving from city to city, town to town, my whole life, I learned never to try to dress like someone else or be like someone else. Never try to blend. Never try to stand out just to stand out. Decide who you are and be that person. That was the way to survive and thrive.

My mom told me we needed to be like every-one else; we had to remain unnoticed. Otherwise *she* would find us. But it was never me who caused a stir or a stink or made someone look twice at me. Mom could not help but call attention to herself. She studied a place, watched how people talked, walked, dressed, ate. Then she recreated herself to be like that conglomeration of people in her brain. And she never succeeded. Something was always a little off. The black nail polish in one town, strange pink lipstick in other, or her fake accent in another.

Not that it was her fault we had to leave. No. Mom was the one who saved us. Who saved me. Every day. It was the other woman, the woman who had been chasing us since forever, the woman who was trying to kill me, to kill us, she was the reason we had to run. You thought there were no crazy people in the world? Wake up and smell the psychos. I've had one on my tail for fourteen years. Maybe sixteen. I'm not sure. I remember a time when I was little, when life was fuzzy cozy, when Mom held me in her arms and sang to me, called me "my little angel." I don't think we were running then.

Hard to see her doing that now. Mom was not what you would call a hands-on mom. She made sure I had the basics though, one way or another. And the basics included breathing room. Actual full on breathing room: life. She kept me alive by keeping us away from the crazy woman. The Shadow Woman. That was what I called her. I didn't know her real name.

I was feeling almost comfy in Phoenix. And then one day, I was walking home from school on one of the service roads that runs behind these big old houses. I liked it there because some trees and the fences made it almost shady. Hardly anyone went down this road except for maids, landscapers, or garbage trucks. Which was fine with me. I was by myself. I was always by myself. Not that kids at school didn't try to be my friend. They did. I never had trouble in that department. But I figured: Why get attached? That led to no good.

So I was walking and thinking about stupid stuff, like how my mom had promised me years ago that we would be able to settle down. She was going to find us a nice little house with a backyard where I could have a dog and a tree big enough for a cat to climb up and get stuck in and then I could climb the tree to get the cat while the dog barked below me, and I'd get stuck and Mom would come up to get me, and the three of us—me, Mom, and the cat—would sit in the tree looking over the neighborhood and be completely happy because we knew we were home.

The house would be yellow. With blue trim. Or blue with gray trim. The color varied, depending upon where we were. When we lived in Albuquerque, Mom decided all the doors would be blue because blue meant good luck and we could use us some of that. I was thinking all this when I saw a man on the ground with a woman kneeling over him. I stopped. I knew that man. He was a homeless guy I'd seen wandering around the 'hood the last couple of weeks. The woman was looking through his pockets. It was kind of a frozen picture, like when you see something you don't want to see and you know you should run but you can't or you don't want to.

The woman looked over at me. Her eyes were black or hollow, and I felt cold right to my heart, as though I was starting to be dead but my mind didn't want to face it. I knew the woman. It was her. It was the Shadow Woman. I had never seen her so clearly before. But I was certain. She seemed frozen in place too. I knew I had to run. I knew it. I didn't want to. I wanted to have the strength and energy and guts to stand up to her, to tell her that she had ruined our lives and that I was stronger than she was now. I could protect myself.

I was going to do that. I was. But I remembered what my mother had told me about this woman. She was different. She wasn't like other women. Or other men. No matter how big or how old I got, this woman would always be stronger than I was. And if she got me, she'd come after my mother next. I had to run if I saw her, my mom had told me again and again; I had to run.

So I ran.

Two

I ran back to the rich people's big house and found my mother in our room putting away laundry.

"I saw her in the alley," I said. Nearly breathless. "She was bent over some homeless guy."

"Did she see you?"

I nodded. "I think the man was dead."

"She probably killed him," she said. "That's what she does."

I didn't ask my mom why the woman was chasing us. I used to. But the story always changed. One time Mom said the woman was after us because Mom had stolen her man. Another time she said I had been a witness to a crime. My mom had what she called a "certain facility" which meant she could make shit up like nobody's business. I wasn't good at that. My face turned red, my palms sweated. So I didn't do it. I kept my mouth shut a lot. When I was younger, Mom used to wonder out loud if I really was her son. "You don't lie, cheat, or kill spiders. You don't even talk bad about people." Then she'd laugh and say, "That means I done good, raising you up to be decent, doesn't it?"

Now she said we had to leave this house and this city. Goodbye, Phoenix.

"Can't we go to the police?" I asked.

"You know better," Mom said. "They would dredge up every little thing I've done and they'd take you away from me. Then I couldn't protect you from anything or anyone."

She was already packing. We could get packed and out of Dodge in ten minutes usually. Five minutes was our record.

"I like it here," I said.

"You want to go with or without your things?" she asked. "We're outta here in about two minutes. You remember what she did to your father." Mom zipped up her bag and left the room.

I pulled my bag out of the closet and started stuffing my clothes into it. I hated this. And Mom shouldn't have mentioned my father. She hardly ever talked about him. Sometimes when I didn't want to leave a place, she'd play the Dad card.

For years she told me I didn't have a father, as though that were physically possible. Then she said he had run out on us. A few years ago I found a photograph of a man in this little box Mom took with her wherever she went. Okay, it wasn't exactly *in* the box. I wasn't allowed to look in the box, so I didn't. Yeah, that's right. I didn't look. My mom deserved her privacy as much as anyone. One day when we were packing in a hurry to leave yet another city, she picked up the box and the lock was off or she'd left it open or something; anyway, a bunch of stuff fell out of it—including a photo. I watched it float to the ground, you know the way paper does sometimes when it falls, as though it is moving in slow motion. Mom and I reached for it at the same time, but I got it. Looked at it. It was a photograph of a smiling man with black hair and dark eyes. I turned it over. Someone had scrawled "Ronald Dare" on the back of it.

I handed the photograph back to my mom. "Who is he?"

She sighed and sat on the floor. She looked tired that day, I remember, like she was sick of running too. "It's your daddy."

"I thought you said he deserted us," I said. "Why would you save his photo?"

She looked at me. "I could tell you I saved it for you, so I could give it to you one day, because even if he was a jerk, you deserved to know who he was and what he looked like. But the truth is your father never ran out on us. Your father loved you very much. He was murdered by *that* woman and people who worked for her. Your father was involved in some shady business. I think maybe he owed her money or drugs or something."

"Can't you explain to her that we don't know anything about what Dad did?" I asked.

"I told you," Mom said. "She's not like other people. She can't be reasoned with. And you were in the house when it happened. I was in the kitchen. She thinks we saw something."

"I didn't see anything," I said.

"I know," she said. "You were too young. I am grateful for that. It was brutal what she did." Mom shuddered. "I don't want to think about it."

That was all she would say then and she still wouldn't talk about it or him, except to remind me that we had to keep running because of what "that woman did to your father."

Mom came back into the room as I was zipping up my bag.

"The cab will be here soon," Mom said. "You sure you've got everything?"

I nodded.

"Aw, don't look so sad," she said. She put her arm across my shoulders. "We'll go somewhere new and exciting! This place was a drag anyway."

"Yeah, sure," I said.

"Tell you what," she said. "You get to pick your own name and one of the places this time." She sat on the bed and patted the space next to her. I sat. She reached into the pocket of her jeans and pulled out a coin.

"I say let's go to St. Petersburg," she said.

"Are you nuts?" I said. "It's almost June. We'll roast."

"All the more reason to go there," Mom said. "No one would suspect it."

"Okay then," I said. "I say Portland."

"All right," she said. "Heads is St. Pete's. Tails is Portland."

She threw the coin up in the air. I watched it slowly turn as it fell. Knew the course of my life was about to be determined by this flip of the coin, as it always was—only my mom usually picked the two places.

She slapped the coin onto her forearm and then moved her hand away.

"Tails," she said. "Okay, Portland, Maine, here we come."

"Not Maine," I said. "Oregon."

Mom stood, picked up her bag, and slung it over her shoulder.

"You know I don't like Oregon," she said. "Too many bad memories. Too much rain."

"A deal's a deal," I said. "That's what you always tell me. I've never been. I want to see the ocean."

"The ocean is two hours away from Portland," she said.

"Okay, then let's stay in some small town on the coast," I said. I knew she would never go for that. It was easier to get lost in a big city than it was in a small one.

"How about LaLa land?" Mom asked. "I bet I could find us another big fancy schmancy house to live in."

I grabbed my bag. "Whatever, Mom. You're the boss. I guess you're gonna pick my name this time, too. Something stupid again."

"Okay, okay," she said. "We'll try Portland." She planted a wet kiss on my cheek. "What a sucker I am for you, my baby."

I wiped her kiss away. "I'm not a baby. And my name is Michael."

"Michael?" she said. "You've been Michael before."

"Yeah, and I like it. That's my name."

"Okay, we'll be Bonnie and Michael Johnson. That's easy to remember. And we're on the run from my abusive husband."

"Oh man," I said. "I hate that tired old story."

"But it's easy to remember," Mom said.

Bonnie Johnson. Mom was always picking some name for herself that didn't suit her one bit.

They were always these cheerful sunny names like Cherry, Angie, Bonnie, Aurora, Blossom. My mom wasn't cheerful or sunny. She tried to be. She tried to be upbeat. I didn't know why she was always pretending she was Miss Funny Sunny.

The doorbell rang.

The cab was here. No one else was home, so I wouldn't get to say goodbye to Melissa or her parents. Not that that was a big deal. I stopped saying goodbye a long time ago.

Mom left the room. She didn't even look around. I did. I grabbed my black leather jacket from a hook in the closet. On the left arm of the jacket Melissa had sewn a tiny pair of black wings. They looked like cherub wings, only without the cherub. I smoothed my hand over the patch.

"Come on!" my mother shouted from the other room. "It ain't like we're running for our lives or anything!"

I threw the jacket over my shoulder and headed for the door.

Three

That's how we left Phoenix. On a wing and a prayer. Is that how the saying goes? We left on tires and a few curse words. We got to the Greyhound station only a few minutes before the bus left for Portland. But we made it.

It all seemed so familiar after that, the same old ride. This time the bus was heading to California. For the first couple of hours, I held onto the leather jacket. Kept rubbing my fingers over the angel wings. My mom had told me many times that I was way too sentimental for the life we were leading. She was right. I shouldn't get attached. Tried not to.

But I was going to miss Melissa. She was a sweet kid. She made the angel wings for me after I saved her life.

It happened only a few weeks after I moved in. We were both standing in the driveway. It was the first time we talked, really. She was saying how one day she was going to paint the bricks yellow, and I liked that about her, right away, that she had some imagination. The driveway was windy, did I mention that? You had to go up and then over a little hill as you came in. As we were talking, I heard a car coming. Or a motor revving. Something strange about it. I shouted to Melissa but she stood so still, like she didn't hear. I pushed her out of the way, and this delivery truck bounced up and over that hill and almost hit me—would have hit Melissa if I hadn't knocked her out of the way.

But it didn't. We were both okay. Melissa skinned up her knees a bit. When I helped her up, she thanked me. The driver jumped out of the truck, ran over to us, and apologized. Something happened as he came up over the hill, he said. The truck accelerated like it had a mind of its own.

"Craziest thing," he said. And then he took the package to the front door.

"How'd you know?" Melissa asked me. "I didn't hear a thing."

"Maybe where I was standing I could hear better," I said. "Cuz I definitely heard something."

After that, Melissa and I were friends. Or something like friends.

I looked at the angel wing patch now. I should have ripped it off before we left. I could have run up the stairs and put it on Melissa's bed in lieu of a goodbye note. I should have left something.

We stopped in Los Angeles to change buses. Mom tried to get me to change my mind and stay there.

"We've never been," she said. "We could become big stars. With your face and my brains."

"Yeah, that's a good way to be incognito, Mom," I said.

I was glad to hear the call to board the bus about 2:00 a.m. Something sad and almost scary about the people wandering around the bus station. Any bus station. Half of them looked stoned or drunk or both; half of them looked afraid of the stoned or the drunk or the both. Except Mom. She seemed right at home in the bus station. In fact, she looked most at home in these kinds of places. As though she was in her element alongside the dregs, the outcasts, the vagabonds—whatever name you want to give them. Maybe I was, too.

I was especially glad to leave, though, because some of the people had started glowing. Yeah, I didn't tell you about that yet, did I? It was this weird visual thing that happened to me. Every once in a while, I would see a kind of dirty yellow glow around a person. When it happened, I'd wipe my eyes, trying to get the film off because that's what it was like: as though the person had a dirty yellow film on them. That never helped. I even had Mom take me to the eye doctor. Perfect vision. When I told the doc what was happening, he said I might want to go to my regular doctor and get a CAT-scan or an MRI.

Then he told me, "My aunt Libby used to see people glow. She called them auras. Saw them all the time. She said that everyone gives off a kind of light, and she was able to see that light. She tried to get me to see them when I was a kid, but I never could. Maybe you're seeing auras. Not that I believe in any of that crap, but you know, who knows?"

That was the end of it, as far as Mom was concerned. I looked up auras but I didn't think that's what they were. For one thing, auras were all different colors. I always saw the same color. Dirty yellow. Sometimes I would see a person with the yellow glow one day, and the next day the person had no yellow glow. That was why I figured it had to be something to do with me, not them.

Anyway, in the LA bus station, I saw three people with the yellow glow. And it creeped me out. Not sure why. Maybe cuz I knew it couldn't be all good to have this dirty yellow glow surrounding you. The glow marked the person. That was how I started to think about it, actually. I'd see the glow and think, "Oh that guy's marked. Or she's a marked woman."

Melissa was marked for a while. Then she wasn't.

That homeless guy in Phoenix, he was marked. Although he was not glowing when the Shadow Woman was leaning over him. Death kind of washed away all color, didn't it?

I was glad to be on the bus and heading for northern California.

I was sorry we didn't go through San Francisco. I liked the Golden Gate Bridge. Have you ever seen it? They have these phones every few feet for people who are thinking of jumping off the bridge. People travel from all over the world to this bridge so they can die. Hundreds of them. Over a thousand since the bridge was built. Maybe because they felt like they had no control over their lives, they decided they would choose the time, place, and method of their death.

We went to the bridge once when I was a kid and I told Mom I wanted to stay there until the Shadow Woman found us.

"We could push her off," I said. Then we would pick up the red phone—I think it was red—and tell whoever was on the other end that another sad soul had bit the dust. Or hit the water.

Mom said, "If it were only that easy. Death doesn't work that way, baby."

"I'm not a baby," I told her. I think I was ten, but still, I wasn't a baby.

But we didn't go through San Francisco this time, and it was a long stinky crowded bus ride up Highway 5 to Oregon. We made it to Portland around nine at night. We quickly left the bus station and went out into the city darkness. It was good to be off the bus finally. A couple of taxicabs were parked out front. To the right of us was a train station. Red bricks. With a clock tower rising up into the night sky. Something about that train station looked inviting, almost homey. I wished we'd take the train more often. Mom didn't like trains. Planes were too expensive and they kept records forever, she said. On a bus, you were a nobody and people treated you like you were nothing.

Sometimes it was good to be nothing.

I glanced behind us, and I saw something move next to the building, like a shadow peeling itself off the outside wall. My heart started racing. The shadow was coming toward us.

"Mom," I whispered. I wanted to scream. I wanted to run. How could *she* have found us so quickly? I stepped in front of my mother. I saw a glow near the face of the shadow. A cigarette.

The shadow came into the light. It was a man. An ordinary man. He smiled, stubbed his cigarette out on the metal trash can, then dropped it in.

"You need a cab?" he asked.

"Sure," Mom said. "Let's live a little."

The cabbie threw our bags in the trunk. Mom looked around.

"It might be okay here," she said. "She'd never guess we were here in a million years."

The cabbie drove us to the address Mom gave him for a battered women's shelter. I didn't know how she knew where to go. They generally kept the addresses of these places secret. Maybe she had phoned someone when I went to the rest room or something. Mom had never been battered in her life. If a man had ever laid a hand on her, she would have killed him, no questions asked. She would have found a backyard to bury him in and planted flowers over his grave. Mom wasn't sentimental. At all.

Okay, maybe she was a bit sentimental. She did have that box with Dad's photograph in it.

Anyway, I didn't like going to shelters. It wasn't right. What if someone who was really in trouble couldn't get a safe place to stay because we were taking up space?

"Mom," I whispered as the cab lurched forward. "Can't we go somewhere else? This feels sleazy. You're not a battered woman."

"No man has battered us," she said, "that's true. But we've got some crazy ass woman trying to kill us, so I think we can hang our hats in a safe place for a few days to catch our breath and figure out where the hell to go next."

I couldn't argue with that.

The cabbie dropped us off at this big old house in what looked like an ordinary neighborhood. We went around to the side door. A woman stood inside the door waiting for us.

"Welcome to Pythia Place," she said. "I'm Therese. We've got beds for you both upstairs."

I was too tired to notice much as we walked down one long hallway, passed by a huge living room, and went up some stairs.

"Bonnie, this is your room," Therese said. "You'll share it with Janice. She's working right now. And then down the hall, Michael, you'll bunk with Bobbie and Sam. Bobbie is about your age. Sam is five. I think they're both asleep, so take the empty bed and try not to wake them up. We'll see you in the morning."

I glanced at my mother. She shrugged. Therese opened the door, and I went into the darkness. I waited a minute for my eyes to adjust. Two of the beds had dark clumps on them which I guessed were Bobbie and Sam. A bottom bunk and a top bunk, on two separate bunk beds. I dropped my bag on the floor. It made a noise—I'd forgotten I had a book in it—and one of the clumps on the bed moved and moaned a bit. Then the clump threw off his covers and sat up in bed.

Must be Sam because he was little.

And he glowed dirty yellow.

He looked around. Didn't seem to see me. Then he lay back down and pulled the covers up over his head.

I hung my head. Man. I was going to have to sleep in the same room as a marked boy.

Never done that before.

Four

I slept like a dead man. When I woke up, I was alone, and the door was closed. I put on clean clothes, got my toothbrush, then left the room and walked down the hall looking for a bathroom. I heard people talking downstairs. Heard children laughing, heard one crying.

I found the bathroom and did what I needed to do. Then I went downstairs. My mom was sitting in the big living room with several other women. Children of various ages ran around them.

"Jimmy Bob can't help himself," Mom said. "His daddy did it to his momma and on and on. But I couldn't let his son grow up to beat on women, too. So I took Michael Lee in the middle of the night, we got on a bus, and here we are. It's not the first time, but I hope it's the last."

The other women nodded sympathetically. I never heard anyone who could bullshit as good as my mom. I believed most of her lies, even when I knew they were lies.

"There's my baby now," Mom said.

Every time we went to a battered women's shelter, my mom inexplicably developed a Southern accent. I have no clue why.

Mom introduced me to the women. She knew all their names already. I didn't remember a single name. What was the point? They would be out of my life soon enough. No sense wasting brain cells on something like that.

"There's food in the kitchen," Mom said. "I'll come with you."

Mom got up and put her arm across my shoulders. Then she led me out of the living room and down a hallway to a big cheerful kitchen. Light poured in through the sliding glass door, making the yellow walls look like they were made of sunshine. Fruit gleamed in a bowl on the table.

A woman stood at the sink doing dishes. Her head was down and her black hair fell across her face so I couldn't see her.

"Boo!"

The yellow boy popped up from underneath the table. He was grinning. I wanted to reach out and wipe the glowing yellow film off of him. I also wanted to get out of the room. I glanced at

Mom, wondering if she noticed anything. She gritted her teeth and smiled. She was not exactly fond of young children.

"Hello, you," the boy said. "I'm Sam. You woke me up last night. I was dreaming of you. You shook me awake and then there you were!"

He held a toy truck in one hand; as he talked his hands went every which way. His hair was curly and brown and looked like it had scrambled eggs in it.

"Hello, Sam," I said.

"Sam," the woman at the sink said, "you couldn't have dreamed about him before you saw him." She didn't turn to us. She talked through the curtain of hair. It made me nervous. I wanted to see her face. Know who she was. Or more importantly, know who she wasn't.

"I did, I did," Sam said. He dropped the truck to the floor. Mom jumped and scowled. She punched her fist in her hand where only I could see it. I couldn't help but smile. Mom could always make me laugh.

"You got something in your hair, Sam I am," Mom said.

Sam reached up into his hair, grabbed one of the bits of yellow, and put it in his mouth. I hoped it was scrambled eggs.

"There's cereal," Mom said to me. "Or I can make you an egg."

I looked at her. She was volunteering to make me a meal? Now that was new. I had been cooking for myself for almost as long as I could remember.

"Don't give me that look," Mom said. "I can do it."

"Yeah," I said. "You need help? You take the pan out of the cupboard. Put it on the stove. Put a little—"

She hit my arm. "Oh shut up," she said, "or I'll have you cook for me."

Sam made a kind of mewing sound then. I glanced over at him. He looked upset.

"What's wrong, buddy?" I asked. He stared at my mother. I wished the dirty yellow would go away so I could see his expression better.

"She hurt you," he whispered.

"No," I said. "She was playing. It's all right."

The woman from the sink was suddenly there, next to Sam. I could see her face now. One side was black and blue. Oh yeah. I had forgotten where we were. The woman took Sam's arm and gave us a dirty look.

"Didn't you read the rules?" she asked.

She led Sam quickly out of the room.

"Oops," Mom said. "I forgot. No PDVs."

"What?" I said.

"Public displays of violence," she said.

"Funny, Mom," I said.

I looked around the kitchen for a bowl, cereal, and milk. Found them. Mom got a cup of coffee and sat at the table. I sat next to her.

"This place is full of losers," Mom whispered. "As usual. But we can stay for a while. I'll start looking for a job today."

"Mom," I said, "do you ever wonder how she always finds us?"

"I don't know," Mom said. "But we've got to make sure we don't do anything that can be traced to us."

We didn't have credit cards. We never used our real names. I wasn't even sure what my real name was. We didn't have phones. Mom never put anything in her name. I had email at each place but once we moved, I never checked that email again. I always opened a new account. What more could we do to stay hidden?

"I should get a job this time," I said.

"Naw," Mom said. "You're a kid. Have a kid summer. I'll work on getting us that house." She leaned against me for a second. "I promised you that and I'm going to deliver."

For a few moments, it felt cozy and soft in that kitchen, like we were a regular kid and a regular mom eating breakfast. I wondered if I should tell Mom that Sam glowed yellow.

"Okay," Mom said. "I better get dressed and

get going. Have a good one. Don't get anyone pregnant or anything while I'm gone."

The moment passed.

Mom got up and left the room. I finished my cereal, cleaned out my bowl, and then went back into the living room. The women and children were still there, still talking. Several of the women looked up at me and smiled. I didn't know what to say or do. I knew I should open my mouth and pretend to be Michael Johnson. Johnson. Could I sound more white-bread?

Therese came down the stairs then and walked over to me.

"Did your mom have you read the rules and regs?" she asked.

"Um, not yet," I said.

"They're pretty standard," she said. "No violence. Respect for everyone. No sexual activity in the house. Also, don't tell anyone the address of the place. It's all here." She handed me a couple of pieces of paper. "Your mom signed them, but I think you're old enough to look at them. Hope you had a good night. Did you get something to eat?"

"Yeah," I said. "Thanks."

She smiled, nodded, and moved on.

I folded the papers and put them in my pocket. I went upstairs to my room. No one was there. Not even the little glowing Sam. I looked around. I couldn't stay here. Not all day.

I grabbed my jacket, went downstairs and out the door. The sun was up, but it was cool out. I was glad for the jacket. I sat on the wide stone steps.

The front door opened and closed. I looked up. My mom and another woman came outdoors.

"Stay out of trouble, baby," Mom said. "I'm gonna find me some work." Her shirt was too tight and too low-cut, and her skirt was too short. She had more make-up on than a clown. Almost. I wondered where she came up with that look. She grinned, then followed the other woman out to her car.

The door opened and closed again.

"Love your mom's outfit."

I turned around. A girl a little younger than I was stood behind me. She wore more make-up than my mom—which was saying something— and her tank top was skimpier.

"Uh, thanks, I guess," I said.

"My name's Julie," she said, "but my friends call me Jules. You say it like diamonds are jewels, but it's spelled j-u-l-e-s. What's your name?"

"Michael," I said. "At least this week." Jules sat next to me. She smelled like some kind of flower—only it wasn't a particularly nice-smelling flower.

"Yeah, we used to change our names, too,"

　　　　　　　　　　　

Jules said. "We don't bother any more because it's usually a different daddy dearest each time."

"What?" I didn't know why I asked.

"Who beats Mom up," she said. "It changes. It's a different boyfriend each time, and they don't come after us. They kick us out, and we end up in a place like this. You too?"

I shrugged.

"I like your jacket," she said. "Looks good on you. All black. Black jeans, too." She nodded. "With a flower shirt underneath the jacket. You're a study in contrasts. What's with the black angel wings?"

I glanced at her. She was the first person to notice the wings. They usually blended in so well no one noticed.

She didn't wait for an answer. "I like 'em. And why couldn't angel wings be black? I mean, birds have black wings, blue wings, yellow wings, green wings. Why couldn't angels?"

"What makes you think they're angel wings?"

"Something about you," she said. "You've got that angelic glow."

Glow? I hoped I wasn't glowing. At least not dirty yellow.

"What color is it?" I asked.

"What?"

"The glow?"

Jules laughed. "You're funny."

I wasn't trying to be.

"You didn't answer me," she said. "What's up with the wings?"

"This girl almost got hit by a runaway truck," I said. "I pushed her out of the way. After that, she called me her guardian angel, so she made me these wings."

"Kind of like a life-saving badge," Jules said.

"I guess so."

She nodded. "I thought you looked angelic. An angel in black."

I wasn't sure why I had told Jules about Melissa. I didn't often tell people about myself. But something about Jules made me feel comfortable right away.

"Did you ever wonder about angels?" Jules asked. "Are they living or dead? Or were they once living and now they're the undead?"

I laughed. "The undead?" I glanced at her.

She rolled her eyes. "Oh geez. That's Bobbie's influence. He's always talking about zombies and the undead. You met Bobbie yet?"

I shook my head.

"He's a kick," she said. "Although his obsession with all that is dead can be annoying. He actually looks for dead stuff."

"Dead stuff?"

"Dead animals on the side of the road," she said. "Things like that. He's hoping to see a dead body."

"Why?"

She shrugged. "Fascination with the abomination."

I glanced at her. She sounded older than she looked.

"Have you ever seen a dead body?" she asked.

"No," I said. "I'm more interested in live things."

"Julie! Wipe that shit off your face!" I jumped as a big woman strode out of the house. Or flew out of the house. Stormed out of the house. She was a force of nature. Big and on the move. She didn't look at us; she kept on walking and talking. "You look like a little whore, Julie. I don't care who dresses like that, I won't have my daughter looking that way. Go wipe it off."

The woman walked down the steps, down the drive, and onto the sidewalk.

"That was my mother," Jules said. "Tina. Typhoon Tina. That's what one of my daddies called her. He's the one who never beat her. But he did leave us."

"Julie Susan!" her mother yelled from down the street. "Get your butt down here. You can play with your friend later."

"Gotta go," she said. "We're grocery shopping. You wanna come? Tina yells at everyone.
It's really funny."

"Maybe next time."

"OK. Later," she said. "Stay above ground."

I laughed. "I'll try."

Then she was gone. I was glad for a breeze
that blew away the stink of her perfume. Cute
kid. But aromatic.

Yeah, I lied to her. I had seen a dead body before. More than once, actually, and I didn't want
to see any more. Everywhere we lived, people
dropped like flies. Mom said that was the way
of the world: death and dying and some horrible
shit in-between. "And we've got to make the best
of that horrible shit in-between," she'd say, and
then she'd laugh and take me someplace to get
ice cream or a hamburger, and we would pretend
we were like all the other people walking beside
us on the sidewalk or shopping in the stores or
walking their dogs. Only Mom said the other
people didn't see the truth of the world: We did.
Because we lived on the edge. Because we had
to live by our wits.

"I saved you," she told me more than once. "I
kept you safe. I know it hasn't been an easy life,
but we've really lived it, haven't we, baby? We
know what life is! That is a great gift."

Now I rubbed my face. Maybe the Shadow

Woman wouldn't find us this time. I wished I knew her real name. I started calling her the Shadow Woman because I was tired of saying or thinking "that woman who keeps following us so she can kill me."

I heard someone laugh. I looked down the street. Tina and Jules had reached the light and were waiting to cross the street. Jules was laughing. I hadn't had a laugh in a while. Maybe I would go watch Typhoon Tina yell at everyone.

I jumped up and ran after them.

Five

Shopping with Typhoon Tina and Jules was not all it was cracked up to be. Typhoon Tina did yell a lot. At everyone. But it wasn't funny or fun to be around. I didn't think Jules liked it much either. When we got to the Sally Ann, Jules and I stayed at the back of the store and out of Tina's way. We pretended to look through a bin of all blue clothes.

"Julie!" Typhoon Tina yelled from across the room. "Where are you? You're getting on my last nerve!"

"If only she had a last nerve," Jules mumbled. "Maybe I can get her to let me go to the library. I'll tell her I need to study."

"Study?" I asked. "You got to stay in school?"

Jules shook her head. "Oh no. School isn't good enough for me. I'll get polluted or corrupted. No, I get homeless schooled. So much fun. Coming, Mummy!"

As Jules hurried across the store to her mother, I caught a glimpse of something over by the dressing rooms. A shadow. My heart sped up a little as I looked in that direction. Nothing. Nobody. Just glaring fluorescent lights.

Suddenly the lights dimmed. I was about to run, but the lights came on again. I looked up. Windows at the top of each wall went all around the building. I sighed. What was wrong with me? Clouds had moved over the sun and then moved away from the sun. Light and shade. Light and shade.

I had never been a jumpy kid. I had always done what had to be done. I didn't like this new jitteriness. Was that a word? If Mom was pretending she had a Southern accent, she would have said I was as jumpy as a five-legged frog.

I breathed deeply. I had to calm down. We always had at least a month before the Shadow Woman found us, usually longer.

I wondered where Mom was. I hoped she found a job. Maybe we would get to live in another fancy house. If Portland had fancy houses. You could find rich people everywhere, though, couldn't you? Just like you could find poor people everywhere.

Jules was coming toward me. She grinned. "Mom said I can go to the lie-berry." That's how she said it: lie-berry. I couldn't tell if she was joking or if that was really how she pronounced the word. "You wanna come?"

"Sure." I wasn't going to stay in the Sally Ann with Typhoon Tina.

We ran outside and onto the sidewalk. Jules looked around and then pointed right.

"This is the Hollywood district," she said. "Isn't that great? We can say we're living in Hollywood. Wouldn't that be something if we were in the *real* Hollywood. We could be movie stars!"

"You sound like my mom," I said. "She wanted to stay in Los Angeles."

"Man, it must be great there," Jules said. "Wouldn't that be the life? If you were famous you'd never have another problem in the world."

I laughed. "Yeah, right."

"What? You wouldn't want to be famous?"

"No," I said. "Why would you want to be famous? You wouldn't be able to go anywhere or do anything without people noticing you and bothering you."

"I want to be noticed," Jules said.

I shrugged. "Not me." I liked to blend. I liked to watch what was going on. See who was com-

                                        Kim Antieau

ing and going.

I followed Jules through an alley that was also the library parking lot and then we walked to the front door of the library. Jules looked at me and grinned. "Here it is," she said. "It's tiny but grand."

She was right. It was a tiny library. Stacks on one side, kids' area on the other. Jules ducked into the stacks and walked through them to the other side. She stopped at the end of them and looked around. Several small rooms with glass walls lined this part of the library. She went to one room, opened the door, waved me in impatiently, then closed the door behind us. A boy with headphones on looked up at us. He was probably my age, shorter, skinnier, with straight black hair that came down to his shoulders. He was dressed all in black. We sat at the table with him. The room was the size of a closet.

"Hey, what's up?" The boy pulled off the headphones.

"Running from da law," Jules said. "As per usual. What are you listening to?"

"Piano Concerto No. 20 in D minor," he said.

Jules grabbed the headphones from him and put them on.

"Hah!" she said. "Liar. This is Mozart's piano concerto in J minor. You can't fool me."

They looked at each other and started laughing.

I couldn't help it. "What?"

"He's listening to Dido," she said.

"Who's Dido?" I didn't usually ask so many questions. It was amazing how smart people thought you were if you kept your mouth shut. Something about Jules made me almost talkative.

"You know," Jules said. "She sings about going down with the ship and never surrendering. She says she's in love and always will be."

"Oh yeah," I said. I didn't have a clue.

"I love the idea of never surrendering," Jules said. "That's me. I'll go down with the ship. I'm in love and always will be." She did a little dance in her chair.

"I like Dido because she's named after a Queen," Bobbie said.

"Yeah, you can relate to that, eh, Roberto?" Jules said. "Well, can't we all?"

"What's with the clown make-up?" Bobbie asked.

"Oh, I forgot." Jules laughed. She started to wipe it off with the palm of her hand. "I was trying to drive Tyrannical Tina crazy, so I caked it on this morning. I thought she'd make me take it off so I forgot all about that."

"Don't try to wipe it off that way," Bobbie

said. He reached into his pocket and pulled out a handkerchief and handed it to her. "You're smearing it all over. You look like a crazy person."

"Yes, Mom," Jules said. "While we're on the topic, look at you two all in black. Goth is so over."

"Black is the new black," he said.

I had my hands in my pockets, so I flashed my jacket open, exposing my blue flowered shirt, and then closed it again.

"I'm Robert Maine," the boy said. He held out his hand. "People call me Bobbie. With an 'i' and an 'e.' The undead call me Robert. What you call me could determine the fate of the entire planet. Or the fate of the three people in this room."

I shook his hand. "Hello, Bob," I said. "I'm Michael Johnson."

"Nice straddle," he said. "But I don't think I'm a Bob. Please tell me I'm not a Bob."

I thought Bob was a perfectly respectable name. I had been a Bob once. The kids nicknamed me Bob 'n' Weave. So clever they were not.

"How'd you get away from Tyrannosaurus Tina, Jewel of the Nile?" Bobbie asked.

"I told her I needed to study," Jules said. "She only went for that because I was with Mikey here. She took one look at him and decided he was a good influence."

I leaned back in my chair. I supposed there

were worse things than being perceived as a good
influence.

"Man, let's get out of here," Bobbie said. "Feel
like a sardine."

I kind of liked the room. I could see who was
coming and going. No shadows. No places to hide.
At least not in this teeny little place.

We left the room and the library and walked
down the sidewalk away from the library.

"Find any undead today?" Jules asked.

"You mean dead or undead?" Bobbie asked.
"I did find a dead bluejay a few blocks from the
house, but it ain't smart to poke around dead birds.
Who knows what they've died from. So I let it
be. I was on Burnside earlier looking for zombies.
Found quite a few. They're starting to blend in
better and better. Warmer weather and all."

I looked straight ahead and wondered what the
hell they were talking about.

Bobbie reached into the bag on his shoulder
and pulled out a sketchpad. We stopped on the
sidewalk and he opened the pad and showed it
to me.

"He's doing a graphic novel," Jules said. "It
is so cool."

"Yeah, it's completely original," Bobbie said.
"There's this undead guy Harlan who is in love
with Joey, who isn't one of the undead, and Joey
won't have anything to do with the undead. He's

                                     Kim Antieau

such a snob. Now Jack, who is also undead, keeps trying to get Harlan to stick to his own kind." Bobbie pointed to the three characters as he spoke. Harlan and Jack had this kind of yellow glow around them. "I was going to call it *Night of the Lavender Dead*, homage Romero, but it takes place over a few weeks. I thought about calling it *Fortnight of the Living Dead*, but that seemed too literary. For now I'm calling it *Undying Love*."

"What is that?" I asked. I pointed to one of the figures. "Why do you have them glowing?"

"Oh, that's a way to let the reader know who's a zombie and who isn't," Bobbie said. "I didn't want flesh hanging off of them, at least not yet, because, you know, that's so unattractive."

"But why a yellow glow?" I asked. "Do you see a yellow glow around some people?"

Bobbie shrugged. "I've never actually seen a real zombie," he said, "so I don't know if they glow. I've never seen anyone glow. I don't think. Why? Do you think it makes them look too hokey?"

"No," I said. "No, they look great."

"Anyway, Jack is secretly in love with Harlan," he said. "It's a kind of undead triangle. Like I said, no one else has done anything like it. Okay, if you don't count *Creatures from the Pink Lagoon*."

"*Creatures from the Pink Lagoon*?" I was

afraid to ask.

"Oh, it's great," Jules said. "It's like *Night of the Living Dead* only it's not in black and white and everyone is gay, even the zombies."

"You two are really into zombies." I said.

"No," Jules said. "That's Bobbie's thing. I go along for the entertainment."

We started walking again. We went by a school. Next to it was a park. Bobbie and Jules stepped off the sidewalk and onto the grass and went into the park. I followed. We went toward a group of huge old trees that all looked like they had breasts.

"I love these trees," Jules said. "Sycamores. They remind me of that statue of the goddess Artemis. They call it the Many-Breasted Artemis."

We sat at the base of one of the trees, each of us with our backs to it.

"I think they now believe those are eggs," Bobbie said. "Not breasts. Either eggs or testicles. They think maybe the people castrated bulls as a kind of sacrifice to Artemis. So they're not breasts or eggs but testicles."

"You're making that up," Jules said. "Now every time I look at her or these trees I'm gonna think of bull balls."

For some reason, this made all three of us laugh.

"So where are you from, son?" Bobbie

asked.

"Everywhere," I said. "And nowhere."

"Enigmatic," Bobbie said. "I like that."

"How long have you two been at the house?" I asked.

"I've been there three weeks," Jules said. "This time. We're leaving in a couple of weeks. Mom found us an apartment away from the most recent bad man, near Pythia Place. It's not far from here."

"This time we've been here two weeks," Bobbie said. "We don't live that far away, actually. My dad is still at the house. Mom goes there once a day and cooks for him. He gets drunk and beats her and tries to kill me and she still cooks for him. I'm torn. Who do I despise more?"

"You're kidding," I said. I thought I had it weird.

"Dad is very old school," Bobbie said. "He hates queers and liberals. Not necessarily in that order. I try to concentrate on the good time."

"The good times?" I asked.

"The good *time*," Bobbie said. "It was one June day. For about ten minutes walking in this park we were all one big happy family. Dad had someone take a picture of us over there." Bobbie pointed. I could see a bronze statue of a girl and a dog. Off to the side was another statue of a man. "With Ramona, Ribsy, and Henry Huggins.

Afterward, Dad went to a bar and celebrated our ten minutes of domestic bliss. Came home and beat on us. Could never read Beverly Cleary after that." He shrugged. "I've only got to make it another eighteen months and I'm gone. I'm trying to become an emancipated minor, but they don't make it easy."

"Your mother should get a divorce," Jules said. "That's what my mother always does."

"My mom would kill anyone who touched her or me," I said.

Oh man. I wasn't supposed to say that out loud.

Jules put her face inches from mine. "So what the hell you doin' in a place for battered women?"

I sighed.

"Back away, Jewel of the Nile," Bobbie said. "Give the boy some personal space."

"You can't tell anyone," I said. See, this was what happened when you talked to people. Trouble with a capital 't.'

"Oh good," Jules said. "A secret. I am so beyondo mondo good with secrets. The secrets I could tell you. But I won't because I can keep them. So what, what, tell us?"

"Geez," I said. "Let me catch my breath. You're sucking the air out of the park."

"All right," she said. "Take your time, new

angel boy."

"We *are* running for our lives," I said. "My father was murdered, and I was in the room when it happened, but I was too young so I don't remember anything. Anyway, the murderer has been hunting us ever since."

"Oh man," Bobbie said.

"You can't tell," I said. "My mom would kill me."

"That would kind of defeat the purpose wouldn't it?" Jules said.

"Yeah, well," I said.

"I guess all that stuff I said about the undead must have hit home," Bobbie said.

I started laughing. I knew he was trying to be serious, but it was funny.

"Why? My dad didn't come back as a zombie or anything," I said. "Hey, what do you guys know about Sam?"

"Little Sammy," Bobbie said. "He's had a tough time. His dad is a drunk, too. His mom isn't much better. Don't you wonder why people keep popping out babies? I'm certainly glad my parents stopped with one."

"Is he sick or anything?"

"Not that I know of," Bobbie said. "Why?"

I shrugged. "Just wondering."

"Why would you wonder that about him?" Jules asked.

"His color seemed a little off this morning," I said.

"Oh, and you're afraid he might be contagious?" Jules said. "A germaphobe. We don't tolerate any kind of phobes around these parts. We are intolerant of phobes." She started laughing as she talked. Bobbie and I looked at her.

"It's good she can entertain herself," I said.

"Yep, that's our jewel," Bobbie said.

"Hey, be nice to me," Jules said, "or I'll come back after I'm gone and haunt you. Or eat you, depending on how I come back. As the undead or as the dead dead." She stopped laughing. "Hey, did you see that?"

"What?" Bobbie asked.

"I thought I saw someone over there, by that tree." She pointed. "She was watching us. When I looked at her, she ducked behind the tree."

"She?" I asked. "It was a woman?"

"I think so," Jules said.

"I need to go," I said.

"Wait," Bobbie said. "Let's see who it is."

He jumped up before I could stop him, and the two of them ran toward the tree. My heart started racing. I wanted to run after them, to stop them, but I could barely move. What would *she* do if they confronted her? Would she kill them? Should I run now to save myself?

No, no, no.

"Wait!" I yelled.

I ran as fast as I could to catch up with them. But they were at the tree.

I got there in time to see a crow rise up from the grass and fly away.

"No one's here," Jules said. "I could have sworn a woman was standing here." She shrugged. "Guess I imagined it. Weird."

"It's cold," Bobbie said. "Let's get out of here."

Six

We stopped at the library on the way back to the house, so Jules could check out a couple of books.

"She'll yell at me not to lose them," Jules said, "but it'll be proof I actually went to the library. Someday I'll make a great master criminal."

"Is that your goal?" I asked as we started to leave the library.

"Her goal is not to flame out before the age of twenty," Bobbie said.

"Hey Michael Angel," Jules said, "weren't you listening before? I want to be a star!"

She whirled around, Bobbie opened the library door, and she danced through it.

At the house, we found Mom and Typhoon Tina staring at each other like two cats getting ready to spring.

"Uh-oh," Jules whispered. "Mommies aren't playing nice."

Typhoon Tina looked at Jules, but she didn't yell. She didn't say anything. She got up, walked across the room, and went up the stairs. Jules quickly followed her.

Then Mom looked at me and said, "Who's your little friend?"

"And Toto, too," Bobbie said.

"This is Bobbie Maine," I said. "Bobbie spelled with an 'i' and an 'e.'"

"I'm Bonnie Johnson," she said. She held out her hand and Bobbie shook it.

"Charmed, I'm sure," he said.

Mom laughed. "I like this kid. We've got a lot in common. Like our names have all the same letters in the same order except two."

Suddenly she sounded like she was about twelve years old or a Valley girl or someone not too bright. I glared at her. She smiled. Sometimes she couldn't help herself.

Bobbie sat next to her. "That's true. What else do we have in common? Were you born in a crossfire of hurricanes? Unwelcomed and un-wanted?"

Mom put her arm across his shoulders. Now she was cuddly mom?

"Abso-freaking-lutely," she said. "The stories

I could tell you. But then I'd have to—"

Don't say it, Mom. Don't say it. Remember where we are.

"But then I'd have to tell them all to you and you'd be bored to death," she said.

"Oh good," he said. "Then I could do research on my zombie comic."

Mom shook her index finger. "No, only if you came back as the undead," she said. "And there's no guarantee of that."

She squeezed him and then let him go. He was smiling like a little kid in love. I shook my head. My mom could charm the scales off a fish. Why couldn't she charm the killer out of my would-be assassin?

Sometimes it seemed like my mom could do anything. Other times it seemed like she couldn't do anything right.

"Come on, boys," she said. Now she sounded like my mom again. "We should probably help out with dinner if we want to eat any."

We followed Mom across the room and down the hall. She was still wearing her skimpy outfit, and she was swinging her hips so hard you'd swear she was tossing something off of them. To the left, to the right, to the left. Boom chicka boom, chicka boom, boom, boom.

"Can she be my mom, too?" Bobbie asked.

I laughed. I wouldn't burst his bubble, at least

not yet. Grass always looked yummier on the other side, didn't it?

We helped make dinner. A big pot of spaghetti and a salad. And lots of noise. My mom was the life of the party. She acted like she didn't even mind the kids running around and screaming and doing other kid things. At least I figured she was acting. Maybe she didn't mind them this one night. In this group of varied black and blue people, Mom didn't stand out. She seemed like one of the gang. Only bigger, stronger. Glowing. Not like the marked boy. Who was still yellow, by the way. No. She looked like she was in her element: tasting the sauce, putting an herb or spice in it, calling to the children to gather around her because she was Queen of Everything—as were all their mothers.

"We are all Queens of Everything," Mom said. "As such, we proclaim you come and stuff your little faces to your hearts' desire. Ice cream for all after, if you finish your dinner and don't barf it up."

Ah Mom. Such a spellbinder.

The only one who didn't seem enamored with her was Typhoon Tina. She got her plate of spaghetti and took it up to her room. Even though that was against the rules.

Not that I was keeping track.

Jules liked Mom, too. She got all quiet around

her and sat at her feet like a little puppy. Bobbie, too. I didn't see his mother. Not that I'd know her. He said she was probably over at his house with his father.

After dinner, Mom and I left the house and took a walk around the 'hood by ourselves.

"I got a job," she said. "I'll start tomorrow. Waitressing. It's a place called the Food Train. It's in this building that kind of looks like a train car but it's not." She shrugged. "The guy says the tips are pretty good. We'll see. I'll start looking for an apartment, too."

"How will we get enough money for first and last month's rent?" I asked. That had been a problem in the past.

"I've got my stash from Phoenix," she said.

Since we got room and board in Phoenix, we had saved most of Mom's salary. We never opened a bank account; Mom kept the money hidden in our room somewhere. I hadn't even known where it was.

"I have a feeling about Portland," Mom said. "Maybe we should have come here sooner. She'd never guess I'd come back here."

She put her arm across my shoulders, just as she had with Bobbie. Maybe Mom was getting more affectionate in her old age.

"Now tell me about your day," she said. "I see you've made some little friends. That's good,

Michael. I want you to have a great summer. Remember not to get too close. We have to be careful what we tell people."

I shook her arm off of me.

"I know, Mom," I said. "I'm not a kid. You don't have to keep telling me these things over and over. I know how screwed up my life is. I know what I need to do to keep it from getting even more screwed up."

I put my hands in my pockets and hurried down the sidewalk, away from her.

"Michael!" she called.

"I'm going for a walk," I said.

Mom didn't follow me. I walked and walked. I was sick of this life. I wanted a different one. I wanted to be rid of this woman who stalked me. There had to be a different way. I didn't want Mom to get killed or go to jail. I didn't want to be put in a foster home. But it was too hard to always be running for my life. To be in fear all of the time. Maybe if I could find the Shadow Woman first. I could explain to her that I never saw anything. I didn't remember my father or his murder. And if my father did owe her money, I'd get a job. I'd work it off. I'd spend the rest of my life working it off. I wanted to stop running. I wanted a normal life.

Shit. I hadn't even been able to say goodbye to Melissa. I wondered what she was doing now.

Maybe in a different time and place we would have become boyfriend and girlfriend. She had kissed me once when we were up in her bedroom, sitting on her bed eating pizza and talking about nothing. She leaned over and kissed me on the mouth. I remember her hair brushed my cheek. It tickled and felt soft all at the same time. I breathed in her breath and her smell. And I smiled. I sat on the bed grinning like an idiot. She laughed and said, "I wanted to see what it felt like." When I didn't say anything, she said, "Aren't you going to ask me what it felt like?"

"I know what it felt like," I said. "Like being kissed by a butterfly."

She liked me saying that.

Maybe some day I could go visit her. Maybe after the Shadow Woman died. She'd have to grow old and die one day. Right?

It was dark by now, and I wasn't sure where I was. I stood in a Wal-Green's parking lot looking at the New Season's Market across the lot. I turned around and tried to get my bearings. I should have been paying more attention. It wasn't like me to get lost.

I wondered what I would have been like if Dad had never died and the three of us had lived a regular life together. Would I have had brothers and sisters? Where would we have lived? Maybe here in this city. Mom never wanted to come here.

Maybe it was because this was where it had all started. I asked her years ago why she didn't want to go to Oregon or Washington state, and she told me she didn't like the rain. Like I believed that. She didn't like the cold either and we had lived in Chicago a couple of times.

I walked to the corner and looked at the road signs. Killingsworth and 33rd. Killingsworth did not sound familiar. I headed south on 33rd. After a while, I went by Grant Park, where Jules, Bobbie and I had been earlier in the day. It looked a little too dark right now, so I didn't cut across it. But I knew where I was now. I got off the main road and started walking through the neighborhood. It was a dark and chilly night. The light from the street lamps pooled beneath them, illuminating a bit of the street and sidewalk but not much beyond that. Ahead of me, coming toward me, was a shadow.

I stopped and stared. Squinted. Was it a dog? An owner and a dog? No, it was upright. But not striding toward me. Almost tentative. Like the Shadow Woman. My heart started racing. I wanted to run again. Like always. Run, run, run.

But I wasn't going to. Not this time. I was going to stand my ground. I was going to ask her why she didn't leave us alone. It was a risk. I knew it was a risk. Mom said she would make me tell her where Mom was. It would be the end of both of us.

I couldn't do that to my mother. Couldn't do it.

I started to back away, and then I saw yellow. A yellow glow. And three shadows stepped into the light and I saw it was Jules, Bobbie, and Sam. Jules waved.

Sam ran toward me. He carried something in his hand. When he got to me, he opened his hand. A bird sat on his palm. Its left wing dangled slightly.

And it glowed yellow.

"It's a male junco," Jules said. "Maybe a car hit it or something."

It was a tiny gray bird with a black head. The line between the gray and the black was so defined that it almost looked like the bird was wearing an executioner's hood.

"I told them not to pick it up," Bobbie said.

"Them?"

"The Jewel in the Crown and the Saminator."

"It's hurt," Sam said. "Can you fix it?"

"No," I said. I looked at Jules and Bobbie.

"He thought you could fix it," Bobbie said. "Something about the dream he had last night."

I sighed. I didn't know what to do with a hurt bird. I gently pet its glowing black head.

"How you doing, little fellah?" I said. "It could

be in shock. Maybe if we kept it safe and warm for the night it might recover. We could take it to the house and put it in a box. Give it food and water. In the morning we can take it somewhere to get help if it's still alive."

"Maybe it'll heal itself," Jules said.

Sam nodded.

"Things don't usually heal themselves," I said. Why was Jules getting this kid's hopes up? I looked at her and realized it wasn't just his hope: She wanted it to survive, too.

When we got back to the house, we found an old shoe box. We put some tissue and a tiny bowl of water in it. Then Sam gently put the bird inside. Bobbie got a shovel and went to the back yard, and eventually brought back a couple of worms.

"Should we grind them up or something," Jules asked, "so the bird can actually eat them?"

"I'm not grinding up anything alive," Bobbie said. "I did my part."

"Let's put them in the box and hope the worms don't eat the bird," I said. "You know, it's probably not going to last the night."

Therese wouldn't let us bring the bird into the house—she caught us when we were trying to sneak it in. But she said we could leave it in the garage. She even gave us an old hand towel to put in the box to keep the bird warm.

Sam didn't want to leave the bird alone. I

told him I would come out and check on it in the night. We closed the garage door so no cats could get in, and we punched holes in the lid and put it over the box.

"Come on, buddy," I said to Sam. "Time for bed." I hadn't seen Sam's mother since we got home, but I figured it must be time for bed.

"Goodbye, buddy bird," Sam said. He lifted the lid and leaned forward. Then he whispered, "Kiss, kiss. Slept tight. Don't let the bed bugs bite. Love you."

Then Sam took my hand, and we left the garage through the side door. Bobbie and Jules followed us.

Sam looked up at me. "I think buddy bird will fly again," he said.

"I hope you're right," I said.

"Knock on my door when you're going down to check on buddy bird," Jules said. "I want to see, too."

Bobbie and I helped Sam get ready for bed. We washed his face. The three of us brushed our teeth in the bathroom together. Then we went back to the room, turned off the light, and got into our beds.

"Good night, Michael," Sam said. "Good night, Bobbie. Don't let the bed bugs bite. Love you."

Bobbie and I didn't say anything at first. I

wondered if he was as surprised as I was.

"Good night, Sam I Yam," Bobbie said. Sam giggled. "Love you, too."

Silence.

"It's a ritual with him," Bobbie said. "Can't sleep without it."

"Night, Michael," he said again. "You can come to my dreams again if you want."

"Good night, buddy," I said.

I dreamed I was very young. My mother held me in her arms and rocked me. She whispered, "My little angel." I couldn't see her face, but I heard the smile in her voice. Then I was alone. And someone was screaming. The sound cut like a knife through my little body, and I shuddered.

I woke up with a start. My face, neck and arms were all sweaty. I coughed and sat up. I had never dreamed that before.

Then I noticed the glowing child standing next to my bed.

"Can we go see buddy bird now?" Sam asked.

Early morning light streamed through the gap in the blinds. I had slept through the night. Which was unusual. Shit. I hadn't checked on the bird. It was probably dead.

"Why don't I go check on it first while you get some breakfast," I said.

He shook his head.

"Okay," I said. "Put on some pants."

I pulled on my jeans. Sam sat on the edge of his bed and struggled to pull on his pants. I went over and helped him.

About that time, Bobbie crawled down from his top bunk and got dressed. The three of us left the room quietly and walked down the hall. I knocked on Jules's door quietly. We waited a few moments; then she came out and we all went down the stairs. Didn't look like anyone else was awake. We went out the side door to the driveway. I went into the garage by myself to get the box and to take a peek before I showed Sam. It was too dark in the garage to look, so I took the box outside. I set it on the cement. The four of us knelt down. Sam lifted the lid off the box.

The junco looked up at us and blinked.

"It's alive!" Bobbie said aloud what I was thinking.

Then the bird stood up and fluffed himself. Then he hopped to the edge of the box and flew away.

Sam and Jules clapped.

Bobbie and I laughed.

"I knew you would fix him," Sam said. "Look, the worms are alive too."

"I'll go put these worms back where I found them," Bobbie said. He picked up the box and walked around the garage and out of sight.

"I didn't do anything," I said. "The bird was probably stunned. I'm glad it's okay."

"Me, too," Sam said. "I'm hungry."

"Yeah, let's go eat."

Sam took my hand and the four of us went back into the house.

It was then that I realized the bird hadn't been yellow any more. When it flew up in the sky, the yellow glow was gone.

I wondered what that meant.

Seven

The next few days passed fairly uneventfully. Mom went to work nearly every day. She came home every night smelling like fried food, but she didn't seem to mind it. I visited her a couple of times at the Food Train. She was cracking gum and jokes, acting like some stereotypical waitress from the movies and TV. You know what I mean. How they're all smart, beautiful, and wise-ass. Mom became all of those things. I never stayed long at the restaurant because I didn't like watching her be something she wasn't. That was the one bad thing about living in the mansion in Phoenix: I was at Mom's job and I saw her put on someone else every day. That's what it felt like to me. Like she got up every morning and put on someone else. She told me it was the only way she knew of getting by, of keeping us safe.

I didn't tell Mom about my scary dream, and I didn't have it again. It was different from any other dream I had had before. It felt more real. Like a memory. I didn't see any more shadows lurking in the....shadows. I started to relax.

A few days after the incident with the bird, Sam, Bobbie, and Jules found me on the front porch sprawled on the bench reading *Crow Girls and the Raven Boy* by Charles de Lint.

"Sam has something to give you," Jules said.

I sat up.

"What's up, buddy?" I asked.

Sam held out his hand. In his palm was a pair of black wings made from cloth. They looked like the ones on my jacket. I glanced down at my jacket sleeve, but Melissa's wings were still there. I looked at Jules. She smiled.

"Thank you for saving the bird," Sam said.

"I didn't save the bird," I said. "He needed a little rest."

"Just say thank you and take the wings," Jules said.

"Thank you, Sammy," I said. I took the wings from his little palm. He leaned toward me and kissed my cheek. I wondered how such a loving soul was ever going to survive the world he was living in.

"Now take off the jacket," Bobbie said. "I bet

I'm the only one who can sew, so I'll sew it on. You want the same sleeve or the other one?"

"Let Sam decide," I said as I shook off the jacket. Bobbie sat next to me on the bench. I handed him the jacket. Sam pointed to the other wings.

"Put it next to this one," he said. "So they won't be lonely."

Bobbie sighed and took the wings from me. "I don't think I can stand all this sappiness."

"Oh, you love it," Jules said. "You're the biggest sap of us all."

"What's a sap?" Sam asked.

"It's something that trees excrete," Jules said.

I looked at her.

"Hey, I like nature," she said. "It is more reliable on most days than the average person, living or undead."

I couldn't argue with her about that.

Jules, Bobbie, and I wandered around Portland most days. Bobbie looked for a job. Jules and I tagged along. Sometimes we took Sam with us if we were going to the park. He loved being with us, and we didn't mind his company. His mother was at the house all the time, not doing much of anything. She was there, but she wasn't all there, if you know what I mean. We went to the Lloyd

Center sometimes to wander around or watch the ice skaters. We brought Sam with us once. He wanted to go skating, but none of us had any money. Bobbie promised to take him once he got a job.

Some days we went downtown to Powell's Books or the main library. I could have stayed in Powell's for days. They had room after room after floor of books. Bobbie went from the manga to the music section and then back again. Jules liked looking at all the covers of the books in the teen fiction section. She'd press her fingers against a face on the cover of a book and say, "I want to look like her one day. Look, see. She's a princess. I bet she doesn't have to worry about anything."

"That's just a model they put on the cover," I said. "She probably has the same kind of worries you do."

"Yeah, right," she said.

We all liked the main library too. I loved walking through those front doors every time and seeing this grand black marble staircase etched with vines, branches, animals—like a tree of life running up and through the whole library. Jules went right into the kids' room and sat down by the papier-mâché tree. I liked wandering around the whole library. I figured you could find out about pretty much anything here. I was tempted to get online and check my email. See if Melissa had written. Wouldn't be any harm in it, right?

But I didn't.

Sometimes after we had been at Powell's or the library, we'd walk or take a bus down to Forest Park. It was the biggest natural urban forest reserve in the country. At least that was what Jules told us.

"Five thousand acres," Jules said the first time they brought me to the park. "You could disappear in here and no one would ever know. You could live here. They found a man and his daughter living here a few years ago. They'd been here for four years and no one ever knew. He homeless schooled her, too. Built them a lean-to, lived on four hundred dollars a month. Seems kind of peaceful here, doesn't it? I might like living here."

We walked on a trail that snaked up and through the forest, next to a creek. I didn't hear any cars or other people.

"It's hard to imagine you living in a place like this," Bobbie said. "You're all city girl to me."

Jules did look a little out of place out in the woods with her red-lipsticked lips, caked on make-up, and short skirt. I had to look away as we went up a steep part of the trail so that I didn't see her underwear.

"I surely can't imagine Tornado Tina living here," Bobbie said.

     Kim Antieau

"Who says I'd come with her?" Jules said. "I'd live here with the birds and the bees and come into town sometimes to see you guys or go to a movie."

"I'd come visit you," I said. "I like it here too."

"Maybe I'll put a scene in *Undying Love* here," Bobbie said. "Joey gets caught on the trail late at night and the zombies come after him, but the undead Harlan saves Joey and he's forever grateful."

"Now I'm going to think of zombies every time I come here," Jules said. "Don't tell me anything else, Bobbie. First the bull balls and now this."

I laughed.

Jules took us to the Stone House. It was an old ruined structure just off the trail. Not much remained except a few walls and steps leading up to the second floor which was open to the elements. It had probably been a restroom once upon a time, but now it looked like the ruins of a medieval house.

"Isn't this great?" Jules ran up the stone steps to the top floor and whirled around. Below us was the trail and just beyond that the creek. Tall evergreens grew up all around us, along with some deciduous trees, the kind whose leaves change in the fall. I didn't know any of their names, but I bet Jules did. The forest floor was covered in all kinds of greenery.

"Wouldn't it be great to have a dance here?" Jules said. "Like a prom. I think it would be fun to get all dressed up and come here. We'd be like princes and princesses in an old fairy tale."

"There are monsters in old fairy tales," Bobbie said. He leaned against one of the ruined walls.

"There are monsters in real life," Jules said. She stopped twirling. "I swear if Mom brings home one more loser, I'm gonna divorce her. She's so stupid about it. She thinks they like her, but then they come after me." She looked away from us. She and Tina were leaving the house in a few days to move into their own apartment.

Jules clapped her hands. "Hey, I just thought of something! Why don't we get dressed up and have our own prom here? We could bring a picnic. Mom's got an old radio cassette player that runs on batteries. We could bring that. We could rent dresses and tuxes or go to the Sally Ann and find stuff. Wouldn't that be fun?"

Bobbie and I looked at each other.

"Come on, guys," she said. "We're all going to be apart soon and this'll give us something to look forward to. We can make a date right now. July fourth. Everyone will be in Vancouver or down by the river to watch the fireworks or hang out at the Blues Festival, and we can come here."

        Kim Antieau

I shrugged. "I've never been to a dance," I said.

"I don't mind a little dress-up," Bobbie said.

Jules clapped and danced around the ruins again.

One day the three of us got on the Max and rode it all around town. We sat together and watched people get on and off. Sometimes we jumped off, walked around a bit, then got on a bus. I liked seeing all the bridges. I'd never been anyplace with so many bridges. The Fremont Bridge looked like a Japanese painting or something, like a giant half-moon-shaped harp pulling the sides of the Willamette River together.

"Are there phones on the Fremont?" I asked Bobbie and Jules.

"Phones?" Bobbie looked at me like I was bonkers.

"Yeah, for people who want to commit suicide," I said. "On the Golden Gate Bridge they've got phones every few feet."

"Really?" Bobbie said. "So you could go there and call anyone in the world? Say, 'hey sucker. I'm about to make the plunge and there ain't nuthin' you can do.'"

"No," I said. "It's a suicide hotline. It goes right to a crisis center so they can try to stop people from killing themselves."

"Does it work?" Jules asked. "I mean, does it keep people from killing themselves?"

I shrugged.

"Some guy jumped off the Fremont a few years ago," Bobbie said. "I remember because my dad asked why I didn't follow his example."

"What'd you say?" Jules asked.

"I said I wanted to stay in the loving embrace of *mi familia*."

Jules and I laughed. If I had to choose between Bobbie's parents, Typhoon Tina, or my mother, I'd take my mom every time.

One day as we were walking down Burnside, I noticed that one of people walking ahead of us was glowing dirty yellow. I glanced around to see if anyone else was glowing. They usually came in bunches. It was like looking for a particular flower out in the woods. At first you only saw one and you'd think that was it. But if you kept looking, the other ones would come into view. Jules taught me that, believe it or not. Up in Forest Park she turned into a little nature nut.

Anyway, I looked around, but I saw just one glowing yellow man.

"I want to follow that man," I told Jules and Bobbie.

"Oh goodie," Jules said, rubbing her hands together. "An adventure."

"Into zombie land," Bobbie said. That's what

     Kim Antieau

he called the part of Burnside where so many homeless people hung out.

We stayed well behind the marked man as he wove between the people gathered in front of a bar that was down the street from one of the homeless shelters. At the entrance to Chinatown, marked by two golden lions on either side of the road, the man turned left. Now we were the only people on this stretch of sidewalk. The man was singing or talking to himself. Jules walked between Bobbie and me and linked arms with both of us.

"Scared, little sister?" Bobbie asked.

She made a noise. "Of what? A crazy homeless person? Pulease. I've seen crazy, I've been crazy, and this guy's an amateur. Do you want me to demonstrate?"

"No," I said. "I want to see what's going on with him without him noticing us."

"Do you know him?" Jules asked in a whisper.

I shook my head.

The man stopped and stepped into a doorway. A few seconds later, we saw his legs on the ground. He was sitting in the doorway. We walked by. I glanced at him. He was drinking from a brown paper bag. He didn't look at me. We kept walking to the building at end of the block. I leaned against the building and watched the doorway where the yellow man was sitting.

We hung around there for about twenty minutes. Jules sat on the sidewalk and watched a line of ants walking across the cement.

"Wonder where they're going," she said.

Bobbie started drawing in his notebook.

"I've added a new character," he said. "Michael the Archangel." He showed me the sketchbook. Michael the Archangel was dressed in black with a huge pair of black wings growing out of his back.

"Not bad," I said. "I like those wings."

"I think he's gonna have superpowers," he said.

"In a comic about gay zombies?" I said. "Does that fit?"

Bobbie shrugged. "I haven't got it all figured out yet."

Just then, the yellow legs disappeared from view. A moment later, the man was walking down the sidewalk in our direction. We all looked away from him as he staggered by us.

"Oh man," Jules said, waving her hand in front of her face. "He stinks worse than I do."

We followed him down the next block. We were still the only people around. The man turned the corner. Then he leaned against the building and vomited.

"Geez," Bobbie said. "I could have gone my entire life without seeing that. Why are we following this guy?"

"I don't know," I said. "Just a little while longer. You guys don't have to stay."

"Like I'm quitting now," Bobbie said, "after all we've been through together. After all the danger we've overcome. I must see this mission to its end."

"What he said," Jules said.

I laughed quietly.

And then the man fell to the ground. Just like that. It was as though he had been held up by a string and someone cut it. Down he went. I ran toward him. I wasn't sure why. But I did. He had fallen face down, and he was still throwing up.

"Oh god," Bobbie said.

"He's going to drown," I said. I turned him over onto his side. "Call 911. I think I saw a phone down the block."

Bobbie pulled a cell phone out of his pocket. "My mom gave it to me the other day since she's living at the house again. Not that you can tell anyone."

I tried to sit the man up. The smell from the vomit was disgusting. I felt like I was going to lose my lunch.

"Don't tell them he's a homeless man," I said. Maybe they wouldn't come if they knew he was homeless. Maybe they would consider him a nothing. This was not a good time to be a nothing.

The man was dead weight, but I moved him so he was sitting up. He had stopped throwing up. I listened to his breathing. It was ragged, but he was breathing.

A couple of minutes later, the ambulance pulled up. Soon after, two police officers on horses stopped. One of them, a woman, got off the horse and asked us what happened.

"He threw up," I said, "and then he dropped to the ground, on his face."

"You saved his life," one of the EMTs said as he looked up at us. "He probably would have choked to death. It's very common with acute alcohol poisoning."

"What's your name, son?" the police officer asked.

Oh no. I hadn't thought of that. The police would want to know who I was. They would put it into a report. Of course, my name was a fake name, so she'd never figure out who I was."

"Bobbie Burton," Bobbie said. "His name is Bobbie Burton."

"You don't know your own name?" The cop looked skeptical.

"Uh—"

"He's in shock," Bobbie said. "Give him a break. He saved this man's life. His father is an alcoholic who beats on him, so now he's living in the shelter over on Duncan."

I didn't think she believed him. But she closed her pad and said, "All right. You did a good thing getting help for this man. You know, the city might want to give you a citation or something."

"That might be fun," Jules said. "Would the media be there? Taking pictures?"

"No, saving this man's life was reward enough," Bobbie said. "We better get back. Thank you, officer. Nice horsie."

"Will he be all right?" I asked the EMT.

"Sure," he said. "His vitals are stable. His color is already coming back."

His color.

I blinked.

The man was no longer glowing yellow.

Had the EMT noticed?

No, he meant his natural color. He was no longer gray.

He wasn't yellow either.

Bobbie tugged on my arm. He was already pulling Jules away. The police officer and her horse watched us walk away.

"Jules," Bobbie said. "Remember Michael can't have any publicity. He's running for his life."

"I forgot," Jules said. "Sorry about that. I guess we'll have to make you another set of wings. You saved that guy's life. You heard what the EMT said."

"How'd you know something was going to happen to him?" Bobbie asked.

"I didn't," I said.

"Why'd you want to follow him then?" Bobbie asked.

I couldn't tell them the man had been glowing yellow. How would I explain that?

We got on the bus and headed back up toward the house.

Eight

Jules left the next day with Typhoon Tina.

"Don't forget me," she said as we all stood on the porch together.

"Forget you?" Bobbie said. "We're going to the prom together. Geez. How soon they forget."

"Okay," she said. "Don't do anything without me."

She gave first Sam a big hug and then Bobbie.

"I think I'll miss you most of all," she said as she hugged me.

"Okay, Dorothy," Bobbie said. "You're not exactly leaving Kansas. You're just a few blocks away."

"I'm gettin' older by the second," Typhoon Tina screamed from the parking lot. "And old age ain't lookin' pretty on me."

Jules ran down the drive to Therese's car. She stopped and looked back at us and waved. Then she got in the car and drove away.

"She's like buddy bird," Sam said. "Flown away."

I ruffled his hair. "Got that right, buddy."

The following day, Bobbie and I were walking around the neighborhood when he stopped in front of a house and said, "I'm getting off here."

"What are you talking about?" I asked.

He set his pack on the ground.

"This is my house," he said. "Therese said I can't keep living at the shelter without my mom. She said she could try to get me into a place for homeless teens." He shrugged. "Mom came over yesterday and said Dad is sober again. He's a nice guy when he doesn't drink. Mom is his loving wife and I'm his smart and creative son. It's only when he drinks that we both become the whores of Babylon. Don't look so worried. I'm still try-ing to get emancipated. And I start my job at the CloseUp this weekend."

"The CloseUp?" I glanced at his house. It was small and shabby-looking.

"You know," he said. "Like 'I'm ready for my close-up, Mr. DeMille.' They show old movies. That's where I originally saw the *Creatures from the Pink Lagoon*. I can get you and Jules in for

                    Kim Antieau

free now. Or at least for cheaper."

"Okay," I said.

"You've got my cell phone number," Bobbie said, "and now you know where I live. Tacky, isn't it? Ah well. We've all got to come from somewhere." He reached into his bag and pulled out a sheet of paper. "Just something to remember me by."

He made it sound like we were never going to see each other again.

I took the paper. It was his drawing of Michael the Archangel.

"You know the resemblance to you is purely coincidental," he said.

I laughed. "Yeah, okay."

"It's been surreal," he said.

I glanced at him. He was blinking away tears. I didn't know what to say. He waved a hand in front of his face. "It'll be all right," he said. "It was kind of nice, the three of us."

"Let's all meet in a few days," I said. "We'll hang out at the library. In fact, let's plan on it. You, me, and Jules. If I'm not at the house, I'll meet you at the central library, bottom floor, at noon on Saturday."

He nodded and blinked rapidly. He grinned. "Yeah, that'll be fun. I'll let Jules know if I see her first."

We gave each other a quick hug. Then Bobbie

picked up his pack and walked down the sidewalk to his house. I watched him go inside and then I walked back to Pythia Place.

Mom was sitting on the porch when I got home. She was still dressed in her waitress uniform. She looked tired. I sat next to her.

"All your little friends are gone, now, eh?" She put her arm across my shoulders. She smelled like fried hamburgers.

"Did you bring me any French fries?" I asked.

"In the house," she said.

I started to get up, but she pulled me back down. "I feel like I haven't seen you in two weeks," she said. "Tell me what's been going on."

I shrugged. "We've been going around town. Bookstores. The library. The park. Stuff like that."

I didn't tell her about the drunk. Or that Sam was still yellow.

She nodded. "So you're having fun?" she asked.

"I am," I said. "I wish Jules and Bobbie were still here."

"You can invite them over for our housewarming," Mom said.

I looked at her. "Which will be when?"

"We can move in Sunday," she said. "I found this nice little apartment. It's not far from here.

　　　　　　　　　　　　　　　　　　　　　　

Still in the Hollywood district. I like saying that out loud. We live in the Hollywood district. Anyway, you'll like it. You'll get your own room. It needs a coat of paint, but you and your little friends can do that."

I nodded. "Good."

"It's going to work out, baby," Mom said. "This time we're going to be able to stay."

She had said that before. But for that moment, I decided to believe her. I hadn't seen any sign of the Shadow Woman. I could pretend for a little while longer that everything was all right.

I had to tell Sam we were leaving. After dinner, he and I took a walk around the block. I told him I'd seen Bobbie's house, and he didn't live far away. Neither did Jules.

"I'm going to leave in a few days, too," I said.

Sam stopped and looked up at me.

"Where are you going?" he asked.

"Mom found us a place a few blocks away," I said. "You can come visit if you want. Maybe your mom will bring you. I can show you my room."

"Can I sleep in your room?" he asked. "Like we do here."

"Maybe," I said.

He seemed reassured by this. He reached up and took my hand again, and we kept walking.

A red car drove by us, stopped in the middle

of the road, and then it began backing up.

"Daddy," Sam said.

"That's your dad?" I asked.

Sam nodded.

I wasn't sure what to do. Was his father dangerous? Was he the one who had hit Sam's mother?

"Do you want to see him?" I asked.

Sam didn't say anything. The car stopped. A few seconds later the driver's door opened and a man got out.

The man was glowing yellow.

"Sammy, my boy!" the man called. He grinned. I kept a hold of Sam's hand. He backed up almost imperceptibly. "I've come to take you home, Sammy!" The man staggered up the slight hill to the sidewalk. He was drunk or stoned. "Come on, son." The man didn't seem to notice me.

I stood in front of Sam. Then the man looked at me.

"I'm this boy's father," he said. "I'm taking him home with me."

And then suddenly, everything clicked into place. I couldn't believe I hadn't put it together before. I knew why Sam was dirty yellow. It all flashed through my brain: I saw Melissa glowing dirty yellow before the truck almost hit her. But it didn't hit her, and her glow disappeared. And the glow had disappeared after the homeless

                                          Kim Antieau

man died. When the bird was no longer in danger. When the drunk was no longer in danger of suffocating. They glowed because they were in grave danger—or because they were going to die. I prevented Melissa from getting hurt. We saved the bird and the old drunk.

Sam glowed yellow because he was in danger.

"You're not taking Sam anywhere," I said.

I sounded calm and firm. I wasn't. I had never talked to an adult like that before.

"He's my son!" the man yelled. "I wouldn't let that bitch keep him from me and I'm not letting some thug like you keep him from me!"

He tried to push me out of the way. Sam started crying. I pushed the man with my right elbow. He stumbled back and nearly fell. He started to come up the hill again.

"I'm not letting you take him," I said. "I don't want to fight with you. You're too drunk to be driving him anywhere."

"Who do you think you are!" the man yelled. He slurred his words. I wondered how he had had enough brain cells to make it here. How had he known Sam was even here?

Just then I saw Sam's mother in the front seat, her hair hanging down over her face.

She was glowing yellow.

I glanced back at Sam. He stood on the sidewalk sobbing. I ran to the passenger door of the car and opened it. Sam's mother looked up at me.

"You've got to get out," I said.

Sam's father was fumbling with the driver's door.

"I can't," she said. "He'll kill me."

"You're going to die if you stay in that car," I said. "Get out!" I grabbed her arm and pulled on her. Sam's father was so drunk he didn't realize what I was doing. He got into the car. He slammed his door shut and turned on the car. Sam's mother got out as he put the car into gear.

"Run!" I said. I picked up Sam, and ran up the hill and onto a playground with Sam's mother close behind me. Sam's mother stumbled. I helped her up and we kept running to the trees on the other side. I put Sam down and leaned against one of the trees to catch my breath. I glanced around. I didn't see the red car anywhere.

"Does he know where the shelter is?" I asked.

Sam's mom nodded.

"Let's go the back way and see if he's there," I said.

We walked slowly back to the house. All of us kept looking around to see if Sam's father was coming back. We cut across a neighbor's backyard and went through the back door of Pythia Place. I found Therese and told her what happened.

"You'll have to leave," Therese told Sam's mother. "We'll find you a place somewhere else. You've put us all in danger by telling him. Get your stuff together, and I'll take you. I'll call the police and see if they can watch the house for a while."

Sam didn't want to let go of my hand, so I went upstairs with him and packed his bag. He didn't have much.

"You be careful, buddy," I told him. I got the picture Bobbie had drawn of Michael the Archangel and gave it to Sam. "Maybe this will help."

Sam hugged my legs.

"Sleep tight," he said.

"Don't let the bed bugs bite," I said.

"Love you," he said.

"Love you, too," I said.

I couldn't remember ever saying that to anyone.

Sam let go of my legs. I squatted so we were face to face.

"You can do this," I said.

He nodded.

We went down the stairs together. His mother looked at me but didn't say a word. I followed Sam, his mom, and Therese outside.

As they walked to the car, I knew Sam was safe. At least for now.

He and his mother no longer glowed.

He was no longer a marked boy.

That night I dreamed my mother was singing to me. When the lullaby was finished. She whispered, "You're my little angel." I reached up and touched her hair. It felt like Melissa's had. As though a butterfly had landed on my hand. I felt so peaceful. So safe and loved. Then I was sitting on the floor playing. It was a hardwood floor. I was putting a puzzle together. Then the screams pierced my ears. The jigsaw pieces turned into rivulets of blood. I tried to pick them up, but my glowing yellow fingers got bloody. Someone said, "You're making a mess, baby. Time to go."

I woke up in a sweat.

The room felt so empty and lonely.

I went downstairs for breakfast. Mom was leaving for work.

"I heard what happened last night," she said. "Don't worry, baby, we're going to get away from these losers in a few days. See you tonight." She started to go out the door. Then she stopped and said, "Oh by the way, Sammy's father was killed in a car accident last night. He won't be bothering them any more."

Nine

My heart started racing. My mother waved and left. I ran up the stairs, went into my room, and shut the door.

Sam's father was dead.

I bet he wasn't glowing yellow any more.

I wanted to run to the morgue and see if he was still glowing. Almost.

But I realized I didn't need to. I knew the glow was gone: Once someone was safe or dead, the dirty yellow glow disappeared.

Oh man.

This was not fair.

First, a crazy woman was stalking me.

And now I could tell when people were going to die.

Was it only when someone was going to have

an accident? What if they were sick?

Oh man, oh man, oh man.

I should tell my mom I knew what the yellow glow meant. I got up and went downstairs, ran outside. She was gone. I could find her at work and tell her.

But why?

She was so happy that our life was going to be normal.

Normal.

My freaking life was never going to be normal.

Because I was a freak, freak, freakin' freak.

I trotted down the street. I kept my head down. I didn't want to see any marked people. Dead people walking. I mean, I couldn't follow them all, could I? I couldn't save them all.

I wondered who told Sam that his father was dead? That couldn't have been a pleasant conversation. What would happen to him now?

I kept walking until I got to Bobbie's house. I walked up the sidewalk to his door and knocked. I squeezed my eyes shut. I didn't want to see any yellow glowing people. The door opened.

"Hey."

Bobbie's voice.

I opened my eyes.

"Sam's dad was killed in a car accident last night," I said.

　　　　　　　　　　　　　Kim Antieau

"Oh man," Bobbie said.

"Let's go find Jules," I said.

"Okay," Bobbie said. "I'll be right back."

I stood on the steps waiting. I glanced around. Trees and houses. Trees and houses. No people. No dying birds. Squirrels. Whatever.

I wondered if this was really why the Shadow Woman was after me. Maybe I had this ability as the result of some government experiment, and my mother had kept us on the run so they could never experiment on me. No, that couldn't be it. I'd only started seeing yellow when I was about twelve, maybe thirteen. Shadow Woman probably didn't even know about it.

Bobbie came out of the house with his backpack over his shoulder. We started walking in the direction of Jules's apartment.

"Everything okay at home?" I asked.

"Dad's sober," he said. "So I guess it's all right. I've got a lock on my door, though, and I can get out the window in about five seconds. I'm not sure I can get emancipated. It's a seventy dollar filing fee. I could come up with that. But I have to show I can live on my own and support myself. I should have $1,000 in the bank. How am I going to do that? Plus, the court prefers if the child—that would be me—has permission from his parents. I guess I can hope I get my comic out there and it'll make me a multimillionaire."

"Yeah, I think there are a lot of comic book guys who are millionaires," I said.

"I think the same ten guys get rich over and over and the rest of us are the ones cleaning up their shit," Bobbie said. "So how's Sam taking the news?"

"I don't know," I said. I told Bobbie about what happened the day before with Sam, his father, and mother. I didn't tell him about the glowing yellow coming and going.

"Man," Bobbie said. "Your nickname should be Lifeguard. You saved Sam and his mom. They probably would have been killed with him. We need to make you three more sets of wings. We can't forget the drunk. I hope little Sammy does okay. He's such a sweet kid."

"Yeah, you gotta wonder how he managed that," I said. "Given his circumstances."

"Look at us," Bobbie said. "We are model citizens. Well-adjusted and well-manicured."

"You make it sound like we're lawns," I said.

Jules was thrilled to see us. She ran out of the apartment. We could hear her mother screaming at her to stay at home.

Jules rolled her eyes. "Run as fast as you can," she said. "Typhoon Tina is on a tear."

We rode the Max downtown. At first I didn't want to look at anyone, but I forced myself. I didn't see any glowing yellow. Did that mean no one was about to die? Could that be it? Or maybe it was gone for now. My "ability" to see the dirty yellow glow around people came and went. That was one reason I had thought something was wrong with my eyes.

Anyway, I didn't see any almost-dead people. Jules talked about the dress she was putting together for our prom.

"I found this amazing evening gown at the Sally Ann," she said. "It has some stains and rips, but I'll fix it up. It's all shiny. Hey, I've thought of a name to go with our prom. Let's call it 'Night of the Living.' Proms always have a title. That can be ours."

"I like it," Bobbie said. "I might have the first comic of the series done by then so I'll premiere it at our prom."

Neither one of us had told her about Sam's father. Not sure why.

We got off the Max and walked to the central library. We each went our own ways, as usual. I stopped and looked at the internet computers. I thought again about seeing if Melissa had written me.

What could it hurt?

I signed up, looked through some books while I waited for a computer, and then I got on and signed into my email account. It was mostly spam.

If the spam 'bots could find me, did that mean the Shadow Woman could too?

I glanced around the room. No one was paying any attention to me. I scanned down the list. I saw "Lissasweet." That was Melissa. My stomach lurched. I had half-hoped she hadn't written. Now I couldn't resist opening her email and seeing what she had to say.

"Dear James," her email began. That was my name when we lived in Phoenix. "Where are you? We were so surprised when we got home and you and your mother were gone. I was afraid something bad had happened. My mom's diamond earrings have disappeared. She thinks your mom stole them. She was going to call the police. I begged her not to. She did anyway. They didn't have any record of you or your mother ever existing. I guess you are an angel, then. If there's any way you can get those earrings back, it would be good. Dad's so pissed he had someone come in and take fingerprints. I haven't heard anything about that yet. I hope you're well. Hugs & kisses, Lissa."

Diamond earrings. I groaned. Could my mother have actually stolen diamond earrings? My mother was certainly capable of stealing, but she wouldn't put us in jeopardy by doing something like stealing.

I clicked on reply, and then I wrote, "Dear

Lissa. Please don't tell anyone I'm writing to you. We are on the run because someone wants to hurt us. They can't know I've contacted you. But I wanted you to know that Mom would never steal from you. I swear by all I know to be true. Yours truly, James."

Yours truly? That sounded so stupid. Like I was writing a business letter.

Who cared? The important thing was that they had to stop investigating us. Besides, it was too late. I had already sent it.

"Hey."

I jumped and looked over my shoulder. Bobbie. I quickly closed the window.

"You all right?" Bobbie asked.

"Yeah," I said. "You scared me."

Jules walked up to us. "It's kind of stuffy in here," she said. "Let's get out of here."

We caught a bus down to Forest Park. Then we hiked up to the stone house. We walked up to the second floor. Jules sat on the floor with her back against the wall and looked up at the trees. Bobbie sat on the half-ruined wall. I leaned against one of the walls.

"You like your new place, Jules?" I asked.

"Oh sure," she said. "Just dandy. Typhoon Tina has me cleaning around the clock. I'm her little slave. I have a lock on my door this time. That's nice."

"You have to lock out Tina?" Bobbie asked.

"Tina's latest daddy dearest," Jules said. She put her head down on her knees. She seemed a little lost today. Sad.

Bobbie and I watched her for a minute. Then Bobbie said, "Hey, did you hear about that guy they found dead in the 'hood? It was on the news last night. They found him a few blocks from Pythia Place. Naked. Really strange. They found his clothes and shoes, even his wallet, but his watch and a money clip were missing."

Jules lifted her head. "Was he murdered?"

"They think he died of natural causes," Bobbie said.

"What's natural about being dead outdoors naked?" Jules asked. "And missing a watch and money clip."

"They're thinking maybe his family hasn't found the watch and money clip at home yet," Bobbie said. "They think he died of a heart attack. He was a fairly young guy though."

"Did you go and look?" Jules asked.

"No, it was all over by the time I heard about it," Bobbie said. "Besides, ever since Michael told us about his dad, I've kind of lost interest in looking at dead people."

"You're not doing your comic anymore?" I asked.

"Oh sure," Bobbie said. "Zombies are differ-

      Kim Antieau

ent. They're undead people."

I smiled half-heartedly. None of us seemed particularly cheerful today.

"We've only got two weeks to our prom," Jules said. "You guys all ready?"

"Almost," Bobbie said. But he made a face that indicated he wasn't.

"I'll find something nice," I said. "Don't worry."

"Now if we miss each other for any reason that day," Jules said, "we'll meet at the trailhead at 8:00. Okay?"

"It's a date," I said.

Jules looked at me and grinned. "Really? Is this a date?"

I laughed. "Sure, why not?"

"Are you my date, too?" Bobbie asked.

"Why don't we all be each other's dates," I said.

"Don't you have a girlfriend?" Jules asked. "The one who made you the first wings?"

I shook my head. "No, she and I lived in the same house. We were friends."

Not certain we were friends any more. Not if she believed my mother was a thief.

Jules pushed herself up.

"All right then," she said. "Let's figure out what music we want for the prom."

*

I waited for Mom on the front steps of Pythia Place. I had to ask her about the diamond earrings. She would be angry with me for looking at my email, but that was water under the bridge.

"Hiya, baby," she said when she came up the walk. She looked happy today, not as tired as she usually was after a day of work. "How was your day?"

She sat on the steps next to me. Today she didn't smell of french fries and burgers.

"I went to the library," I said, "and I checked my email. Before you get all huffy about that I want to tell you that Melissa sent me a message. She said a pair of her mom's diamond earrings went missing when we left. They called the police and everything. Mom, they could be after us."

"I didn't steal any earrings," Mom said. "She was always losing those damn things. They were so tiny. Last time she lost them, I found them in her husband's tie clip box. I wouldn't steal from them. They were good to us. But more than that, I wouldn't do anything to get the police looking for us."

"I thought so," I said. "I told her you didn't do it."

"Really?" Mom said. She smiled. "It's good to know you have faith in your dear old mom. I'm off tomorrow. It's moving day. My boss says he has an old junker I can buy from him, cheap. So we'll have wheels soon. He'll keep it in his name. He didn't care as long as I paid the insurance premium. Man. I need a shower." Mom leaned on me to push herself up. "You delete that email account as soon as you can. All right?"

"Okay," I said.

She went into the house.

I was surprised she wasn't angrier about me contacting Melissa. I wasn't going to question it. All that mattered was that she didn't steal the earrings. Now I had to get Melissa to stop the police investigation.

I checked my watch. The library was still open. I jumped up and ran down the steps and onto the sidewalk. I half-ran half-walked to the library where Jules had taken me to meet Bobbie a couple of weeks ago. Had it only been that long? It felt like I had been here forever, known Bobbie and Jules my whole life.

One of the internet stations was open, so I got on right away. I logged onto my email account and sent a message to Melissa. I told her where to look for the earrings. I ended with, "Please stop the police investigation. It's dangerous to us."

This time I signed the message, "Luv, Michael."

I sent it. Then I was going to delete the entire account. That was what my mom wanted me to do. She thought that was the safest thing. I hesitated. I wanted to make certain they found the earrings. I wanted to make certain the police were not after us.

So I didn't delete it.

The sun was setting by the time I got out of the library. Everything was in twilight. I put my hands in my pockets and hurried toward Pythia Place. I didn't like this time of night. Nothing seemed as it should be at dusk. Or something. Maybe it was that I couldn't see well at twilight. Could anyone?

I walked quickly. I thought I heard footsteps behind me. I stopped and looked. Didn't see anyone. Kept walking. I heard it again. Soft footsteps. Almost as though a cat was following me. I walked faster. The sound quickened, as if whatever it was was hurrying to keep up with me. Maybe even go a little faster.

Soon it would overtake me.

What if it was *her*?

Was she going to kill me now?

I started running. I looked down at my hands to see if they were glowing. If I was in danger, would I glow? I had never glowed before.

Wasn't glowing now.

Maybe it was like smelling your own stink. It was nearly impossible.

Or was it?

I could still hear the sound. Someone was

behind me.

I veered off the sidewalk and fell into a bush.

A man ran by me. A jogger.

"Shit," I whispered. I tried to catch my breath.

Then I saw something across the street from me. Standing in the dusky light. Hands in her pockets. Looking straight at me. Was it her?

I stood still. I breathed deeply. I looked into the darkness.

Suddenly a street lamp came on, directly over the sidewalk across the road from me.

No one was there. Just empty space.

I ran all the way back to Pythia Place.

Ten

Mom and I picked up the blue bomber the next day. That's what Mom immediately named the old station wagon. It looked like the kind of car a psycho would drive. But it worked, and it carried us and our meager belongings to the new apartment. We went to the Sally Ann and got a kitchen table, chairs, a couch, and a couple of dressers. We picked out flatware and dishes. Then we got two new mattresses from a department store.

Mom and I had fun putting everything in place. The next day, Jules and Bobbie came over and we painted one of my walls a kind of rusty cinnamon color. I think we got as much on us as we did on the walls. We laughed at Bobbie's corny jokes, and Jules twirled around the room, paintbrush in hand.

Mom picked up pizza and pop for us. We all sat around the table laughing and eating. Mom seemed happy. She even wiped paint off of Jules's cheek. Jules got still when Mom touched her. She closed her eyes and let Mom gently wipe the paint off her face.

"All done," Mom said.

Jules opened her eyes and smiled. "Thanks." She reminded me of Sam for a moment.

Later, Jules and I walked Bobbie to the CloseUp. He went to work behind the concessions counter. Jules and I went inside the theater and watched *Invasion of the Body Snatchers*. The original. Jules hunkered down close to me during the scary parts. We ate real buttered popcorn from a box we held between us. Bobbie came and sat with us for the last half 'n' hour of the movie.

When it was over, Bobbie stayed to clean up. Jules had to get home, so I said I'd walk her.

"That was a sad movie," she said once we got outside.

"Sad?" I said. "That's not the word I'd use. It was kind of scary, knowing that people can change like that. Become walking zombies. I wasn't quite sure why they all had to be alike, why they all had to act the same."

"Because that's what the world wants," Jules said. "It wants us all to be alike. Think of the advertising we see all day. They're selling the perfect human being. Their version of a perfect human being. You can't become that perfect being without buying all of their crap. Pretty soon we believe that we're nothing because we aren't like those perfect human beings."

"Wow," I said.

"Yeah, I'm not as dumb as you all think I am," Jules said.

"I've never thought you were dumb, Jules," I said. "I'd never use that word to describe you."

"How would you describe me?"

"Funny," I said. "Smart. Pretty. Energetic."

Jules laughed. "Okay, I like that."

As we crossed the street, Jules took my hand. We walked down the sidewalk hand in hand.

"The woman in the movie changed," Jules said. "She became one of them even though she didn't want to. Even though they loved one another. It wasn't enough. Love was not enough."

"Most of the time it isn't," I said. "My mom loves me, but that doesn't mean we have a great life."

"But you've got a life," Jules said. "She did do that for you."

"Yep."

"Michael," Jules said. "Let's be boyfriend and girlfriend."

"We are friends," I said.

"You know what I mean," she said.

I sighed. Yes, I knew what she meant.

She swung our hands back and forth.

"You and Bobbie are my best friends," I said. "I've never had best friends before. I like it."

"So you think of me as a friend," Jules said. "Not a girlfriend. You don't want to kiss me or anything."

"I guess I don't think of you that way," I said.

"Do you think of Bobbie that way?" Jules asked.

"No," I said. "I think I've been on the run so long that I haven't thought of anyone that way."

Except maybe Melissa. A little bit.

"Can we hold hands now anyway?" she asked. "Like a brother and a sister."

I wasn't sure brothers and sisters held hands. What did I know? I didn't have any siblings.

When we were about a block from Jules's house, she slowed down.

"I don't want to go home," she said. "I thought it would be so much better once we had our own place."

"It's not?" I asked.

"She started seeing that asshole Peter again," she said. "He's the guy who beat her up. He's the guy who kept coming into my bedroom when I was sleeping. I'd wake up and he'd be sitting there. Doing who knows what."

"Is he staying at your apartment?" I asked.

"Not yet," Jules said. "She's so stupid. She keeps doing the same thing over and over. Just like I keep thinking it'll be better over and over. I'm not going to put up with it again. It happened before."

"What?" I asked.

"One of her boyfriends getting after me," she said. "More than once. They're so much bigger than I am. I can't fight them off. I can't do it."

"If you ever need a place to stay," I said, "come over to our place. I'll sleep on the couch. You can stay in my room."

We had reached her apartment building.

"You are a good man, Michael the Archangel," Jules said.

"I don't even know what an archangel is," I said.

"I think he's a rich angel," Jules said. "He lives in a nice house, has nice clothes, plenty of food."

I laughed. "I can see why you got us confused."

Jules let go of my hand. She reached up and kissed my cheek.

She smelled like tulips.

It was kind of nice.

"Night," she said. She waved and walked up to the apartment.

As I watched her go inside, I realized I would do anything for her. Or for Bobbie. Sam. My mom. I would lay down my life for each and every one of them.

I guessed that was what they called love.

Probably be better to figure out how to save them without actually having to die myself.

I smiled and started walking home.

Why did I think any of them needed saving? It wasn't my job to save them or the world.

Was it?

I liked our new apartment. I liked our new life. Some nights Mom and I sat together on the couch and watched television or played cards. A couple of times Bobbie and Jules came over and played cards with us. Mom was good at cards. Good at reading people. She always knew when Bobbie was bluffing, which was almost always. And anyone could tell what Jules had in her hand. She moaned when it was a lousy hand and laughed when it was a good hand.

I kept having that dream. The one where I am older than I should be, four maybe, and my mother is calling me "my little angel," and then the screaming. I always wake up in a sweat. Each time I had it, it was more vivid. This last time my mom had black hair. Soft black hair.

I'd never seen my mother with black hair.

Blonde. Red. Brown. Even purple once. But I didn't remember black. Maybe because it was her natural color.

I didn't ask her.

One afternoon Jules took Bobbie and I to Buffalo Exchange, Red Door, and another Sally Ann in search of appropriate prom attire. None of the places had much for men. Finally we found some old tuxes, probably from a wedding, it looked like. Bobbie and I both wanted the black tux, but it didn't fit him. He had to choose between a pink tux and a green one.

"Stereotype or zombie colored," he said. "Stereotype or zombie. Hmmmm."

Finally he went with pink.

"Ahhhh," Jules said. "My boys. Michael bad in black; Roberto pretty in pink."

Bobbie found a pair of alligator boots to go with his tux.

Afterward, we headed for the library.

When we reached the central library, Jules said, "I need to go. I'm meeting some friends down by Pioneer Square."

"Friends?" Bobbie said. "You have other friends? How dare you!"

Jules laughed. "They're this group of homeless kids," she said. "I like them. I can relate. Mom and I flew the sign some last year, mostly at the ramp off 33rd. There's a real art to what you put

                    Kim Antieau

on your sign, you know. A little humor gets you more licks. I got more licks than Tina ever did, no matter what the sign said. They didn't want to give Momma nothing. I could make a living out there on my own. I don't need her."

Bobbie and I glanced at each other. Momma? We'd never heard Jules call Tina that before. And she seemed to be rambling a bit.

"You'll have to meet my friends sometime," Jules said. "They call themselves a family. This one guy is kind of in charge, but he's nice about it."

"Don't you want to go to a movie or something tonight?" Bobbie asked.

"Another night," she said. "It's all good."

She kissed first Bobbie and then me on the cheek. Then she left us alone in front of the library.

"She's been acting kind of strange lately," Bobbie said. "I saw her the other day and she looked high."

"She'll be all right," I said.

We went into the library. I decided to check my email and see if Melissa had written back. Bobbie sat at one of the tables drawing while I got on the internet.

I got into my email.

Found a message from Melissa.

I clicked on it to open it.

Just then the lights grew dim in the library. I looked around. No one else seemed to notice it was nearly dark. Except someone on the other side of the room by the manga. She was looking at me. Walking toward me. Was it *her*?

I squinted.

Why didn't I run?

The lights came back on. I blinked.

The woman wasn't there. Everyone and everything was as they had been.

Man.

Getting crazy in my young age.

I opened Melissa's email.

"Dearest James: I found the earrings. Just where your mom said they were! My father called the police and told them it had all been a big mistake. Remember I said they took fingerprints? They found mine, my parents, some of my friends, but they didn't find your mother's. Strange, isn't it? The police would like to talk to you if you ever come back. They said they did find one set of fingerprints. They were the fingerprints of a Michael Dare. He went missing twelve years ago after his parents Ronald and Elizabeth were murdered."

Eleven

I didn't see any of the rest of the message after that. It felt like the floor fell away. I was dizzy. Groggy. Like I was going to be sick. Bobbie must have noticed because he was suddenly next to me.

"Michael," he whispered. "What's going on?"

I couldn't talk. I pointed to the email.

Bobbie read it. "Peter, Paul, and Mary! I can't believe this. What does it mean?"

He pulled up a chair next to me.

"Have you ever looked up your father's murder?" Bobbie asked. "I mean, have you done any research on it?"

"No," I said. It had never occurred to me. Dad was dead. What else did I need to know? Plus I hadn't known his name.

Bobbie pulled the keyboard to him and googled my parents' names along with the word "murder." He got several hits. He opened an article in the *Oregonian*. We sat next to each other and read.

"It happened here in Portland," Bobbie said. "Did you know that?"

I shook my head and read the rest of the article. Ronald Dare had been a well-respected lawyer, Elizabeth a school teacher. Their child Michael had been ill just before the murders.

Mur*ders*. Plural. Why did they think my mom was murdered?

"Look," Bobbie said. "The housekeeper and little boy disappeared at the time of the murders. They didn't know if the housekeeper kidnapped the little boy or if the boy and the housekeeper were dead, too. The little boy is you. Michael, you're one of those kids on a milk carton."

"Scroll down," I said. "I want to see if there are any photographs."

Bobbie stopped scrolling when he reached a photograph of the front of the house. There was also one of my father, Ronald Dare. He looked like he did in the photograph my mother had. Next to him was a photograph of my mother, Elizabeth Dare.

Only it was not a photograph of my mother, not the mother I knew. Elizabeth Dare had black hair, a big beautiful smile, and a wide nose.

My mother looked almost the exact opposite of that. Could they have mixed up her photograph with the housekeeper's? Maybe the Shadow Woman and the thugs had killed my dad and the housekeeper and the authorities thought it was my mother.

My heart was pounding in my ears. I felt like there was an ocean in my ears. What did this mean? What? What? I couldn't think.

Bobbie glanced at me. "Did your mom have plastic surgery?"

"Not that I know of," I said. "Look at the other articles. I can't concentrate. Did they solve the case?"

I leaned my arms on my thigh and put my head down. Had to stop the spinning. Had to stop the roar in my ears.

The screaming. I kept hearing the screaming.

I could feel my blood pulsing in my veins.

After a couple of minutes—or a couple of hours—Bobbie said, "No, man, I don't think they did. They never found the housekeeper or the boy. You. Both of your parents had relatives in town. None of them could figure out why anyone would ever kill them. They were well-loved."

"I gotta get home," I said. "I gotta find out what's going on. Bobbie, you can't tell anyone.

Not a word of this to anyone. Not even Jules. And don't let on to my mom that you know any of this."

"Of course not," Bobbie said. "Come on. I'll go with you."

I made a copy of the first article. Then Bobbie and I got on the Max train and went across the river. Several of the people on the train were glowing dirty yellow. I wondered what I should do. Should I follow them? Tell them to go to a doctor or watch out for drunk drivers and runaway trucks? What? What the hell was I supposed to do? Was I supposed to try and save them all because I now knew they were going to die? But wasn't everyone going to die one day?

And I didn't care. I had to find out. Who. I. Was.

Bobbie and I hardly said a word all the way to my apartment. I left him on the sidewalk.

"Stay above ground," Bobbie said.

"Always," I said.

Then I went into the house. Mom was sitting at the table drinking a cup of tea and doing the crossword. I could barely breathe.

I stood over her and dropped the copy of the newspaper article on top of her crossword puzzle.

She gasped.

"Don't lie to me," I said. "I want to know

                               Kim Antieau

exactly what this means.”

“How did you find out?”

“What difference does it make?” I asked.

“I want to know.” She stared at the paper and didn’t look up at me.

“The police took fingerprints at Melissa’s house when they thought you took the earrings,” I said.

“They found the earrings, didn’t they?” she said. “I told you I didn’t take them.”

“They didn’t find your fingerprints,” I said, “but they found mine. They want to talk to me since apparently I was abducted twelve years ago. You’re not my mother, are you?”

“Of course I’m your mother!” she said. “I’ve raised you. I’ve kept you safe. You were sick, you know. See, they say that here. I took you to the doctor that day and got you an antibiotic. Your parents didn’t believe in doctors, but I took you, because I knew you were in trouble. When we got back to your house, your mom and dad were dead. *She* had murdered them.”

“It doesn’t say anything in here about my father being involved in anything illegal or shady,” I said. “Everyone said they were good parents and good people. Why did you tell me all that crap about Dad being killed because he was doing something illegal?”

“I don’t know!” Mom said.

She looked up at me. She had tears in her eyes. I had never seen her cry before.

"I loved you so much," she said. "I knew I should have called the police and let you go to one of your relatives. But I was so afraid that she'd find you and kill you."

"Why?" I said. "It doesn't make any sense. I wasn't in the house when they were killed, according to you. Why would she want to hurt me?"

"I don't know," Mom said. "She's crazy. Maybe I loved you too much. I wanted you for myself. I thought only I could protect you. She's still out there. Baby, I did it for you."

She put her hand on my arm. I moved away from her.

"You shouldn't have taken me," I said.

"They were religious nuts!" she said. "They didn't believe in antibiotics. You would have died. I know it. As soon as you got the medicine you needed, you got better. Your relatives would have let you die, too. I saved your life. Look around. Do you think I wanted this life? I chose it because I loved you. I wanted to make a good life for you."

"It's not working, Mom," I said. "Or whatever your name is. It's not a good life. I see killers around ever corner. This is the first time I've ever even had any real friends."

"That's because it's all starting to be good for

us," Mom said. "It's going to be all right. I know it's terrible learning your biological mother was murdered. But does it change anything now? I took you to protect you. You still need protecting and I'm still willing to do that. I love you, baby, and you love me. What else do we need?"

"More than this," I said.

I didn't know what to do or what to think. I left the house and walked for a long time. I ended up at the CloseUp.

"What'd your mom say?" Bobbie asked. He handed me a box of chocolate covered raisins. "It's on me," he whispered.

"She admitted it," I said. "She said she took me to save me from the murderers. She could have told me! She shouldn't have lied to me all these years."

"I know it's bad," Bobbie said. "I know it's awful. But at least she isn't trying to kill you."

"Is your dad after you again?" I asked.

"Not lately," Bobbie said. "Not ever again. I'm out of there if I smell even a whiff of hatred or alcohol. Go on in. I'll join you later."

I sat in the middle of the theater with my box of raisins. People sat behind me and in front of me. All around me. I felt alone and lonely. My parents were dead. Both of them. Someone had murdered them. I had been running around the country with someone who wasn't even related to me.

The movie was *Invasion from Mars*. It was the one where a boy sees a light in the field one night. His father goes out to investigate. When he comes back, he looks like the same man but he acts completely different. After a while most of the adults in the movie begin acting like zombies.

It was creepier to me than *Invasion of the Body Snatchers*. To be a child and know the truth of things yet not be able to get anyone to listen.

For some reason that hit close to home.

Bobbie sat with me for the last part of the film. He ate the rest of the chocolate covered raisins.

At the end of the film, the boy was reunited with his parents. And they were normal again.

They were alive.

Lucky boy.

When the movie was over, Bobbie and I went into the lobby.

"What are you going to do now?" he asked.

I shrugged. "What else can I do?" I said. "I guess I'll go home to my so-called mother."

"Hey, let's walk home together," Bobbie said. "Another guy was killed last night."

"What are you talking about?" I asked. I leaned on the counter while he and some other guy cleaned up the concession area.

"Didn't you hear?" Bobbie said. "Another guy died. At first they thought it was from natural causes again. But he was missing some things, too.”

“I don’t get it,” I said. “Either he was murdered or he wasn’t.”

“I don’t know what to tell you,” Bobbie said. “But it makes me a little nervous. I’ve gone from ambulance chaser to wimp.”

Bobbie and I left the movie theater together and headed toward his house.

“Hey, you’ll have to walk home alone after you drop me off,” Bobbie said. “That doesn’t seem right.”

“I’m not worried,” I said.

We stayed on the well-lit streets. I knew which ones they were. I always did. Wherever we went, I knew how to stay out of the shadows.

But the last block or so only had a couple of street lights. Bobbie and I hurried down these sidewalks.

“I hear someone behind us,” Bobbie whispered.

We stopped and listened.

Nothing.

We started walking again.

Tap, tap, tap.

Just like the other night.

Only then it had been a jogger.

I glanced behind us.

Citified darkness. Light where the street lamps were; darkness like a curtain beyond that.

Bobbie and I kept going.

We finally made it to his house.

"Why don't you stay here," Bobbie said. "It's weird what's been happening. This used to be a safe neighborhood. We never had people dying naked in the streets before." He shivered.

"Don't worry about me," I said. "I'll get home safe."

Bobbie nodded. "All right," he said. "Stay above ground."

"Yeah, you too."

I watched Bobbie go into the house. Then I looked around. I didn't see anyone. I wondered if the Shadow Woman was out there. This was how it usually started: Dead people began showing up wherever we lived. And soon I'd spot her. Then I'd tell Mom and we'd be on our way again.

Mom.

Not Mom.

Was that what I should call her now? Not Mom?

My entire life had changed in an instant.

Again.

I ran until I was out in the open, out in the light.

When I got home, Mom was waiting for me.

I didn't say anything. I went into my room and closed the door.

Twelve

Mom made breakfast for me the next morning. I ate it, and then I left. When I came home, she made me dinner. She talked about her day. I got up and went into my room. She bought me a little stereo. I turned it up so I couldn't hear her moving around the apartment.

I kept dreaming. People were screaming.

For several days, I wandered around Portland. The dirty yellow glowing people were back. Here and there and everywhere. I thought about picking one and following him or her. Maybe I could make a difference in their lives. But there were too many of them. How could I ever chose?

Sometimes I went into the library and looked up the articles about the murders of my parents. I wanted to find out something about them. The stories were all about how they died. I wanted to know how they lived. Had they loved their little boy? Had they had dreams of his future?

Of my future.

My mom had lied about so much.

What else was she lying about?

Bobbie was working a lot, and Jules was hardly ever home. I started to feel alone again. Mom wanted to take me to the movies and dinner. She kept asking me. Finally I agreed to go with her. We sat in the big theater at the Lloyd Center. They had a special showing of *The Wizard of Oz*. It was the first time I had ever seen the movie.

I wished I had a dog. And a wizard. Maybe ruby slippers that I could click together to take me back home.

Wherever that was.

"Which character do you think I am?" Mom asked. We shared a box of popcorn.

"The Wicked Witch of the West," I said.

"Really?" she said. "I think I'm more like the Wizard."

"He's a man behind a curtain," I said.

"I'm just a mom behind a curtain," she said.

"I'm the Tin Man," I said.

"Looking for a heart?" she asked. "No, I don't think so. You've already got one. You're Dorothy. You're Dorothy if Dorothy was a boy. And I'm Toto."

I laughed. "Okay, Toto."

That was a good night.

The others weren't so good.

I found the address of the house where I used to live in the paper. So I went there one afternoon. Took a bus partway and walked the rest. It was a brick house. Two-story. With a lawn out front. Looked like a yard in the back with a couple trees in it.

I stood for a long time looking at it. Trying to imagine what my life would have been like. I could almost hear them. Hear us. Laughing. Them running after me as we played. Them taking me to school. Me talking to Dad about my first crush. Or would I have talked to Mom? My real mom. Would they have given me advice about love? About school? About life and death?

I wanted to cry. I wanted to sit down on the ground and sob. I didn't. I walked away. I kept walking until I got to Forest Park. I went up the trail to the Stone House. I walked up the stone steps to the second floor. I sat on the floor and put my head in my hands. I was shivering.

I felt a hand on my shoulder.

I jumped. Moved away.

"It's me," Jules said. "You act like someone's after you. Oh wait, I forgot. Someone is after you." She giggled.

It wasn't a normal giggle. She was drunk or

high.

Or something.

"Hi, Jules," I said. "Where you been?"

"Hanging out," she said. "Flying the sign most days lately."

"You stoned?"

She laughed. "Gotta do something," she said. She threw her hands up in the air. "It's all too surreal for me."

"I thought you said you'd never surrender," I said.

"Who says I'm surrendering?" she said. "I'm going down with the ship." She laughed again. "Hey, it's all good. I was trying it out."

She sat next to me and leaned her head against my shoulder. "Do you remember ever feeling safe?"

"Yeah," I said. "Once. I remember my mother holding me and singing to me and calling me her little angel."

My real mother.

That's right. That was a memory of my real mother. Her holding me, her loving me. I had been safe.

And then everything had changed.

"Do you think there are such things as angels?" Jules asked. "I mean, do you think someone or something is looking after us?"

"No," I said. "We have to be our own guardian

angels. We have to look out for each other."

She sighed. "Yeah, I was afraid of that."

She moved away and pushed herself up. I stood too.

"I'll be here Friday," she said. "You too? Be here or be square. Michael the Archangel."

I put my arms around her. Wasn't sure why. I just did it. She stood still for a moment, and then she returned the embrace.

"Stay above ground," she whispered.

"Yeah, you too," I said. "Come over to our place anytime. Remember, you can stay with us."

She nodded. Then she ran down the steps. In another moment she was on the trail and heading away from me. She slipped a little on the muddy path. Laughed. Kept going.

I shook my head. What was happening? Everything had seemed perfect for about three weeks. My version of perfect. Now it was all falling apart.

And I knew it was going to get worse.

I just had a feeling.

A couple days later, Bobbie and I went to the central library. I stood on the second floor staring out the window while Bobbie looked something up on the catalog. People walked by on the sidewalk down below. Cars went by. The light turned red and several people crossed the street.

One of them was glowing dirty yellow.

"Hey, there's Jules," Bobbie said. He stood next to me now.

I squinted.

My heart started to race.

It was Jules. *Jules*. She was a marked girl.

Jules was glowing yellow.

"We've got to catch her," I said.

I ran from the room, down the huge staircase, across the lobby and out the door. I looked to the right which was the direction she had been headed.

No Jules. I ran to the corner and looked up and down the streets.

Where had she gone?

Bobbie was beside me.

"You go that way," I said. "I'll go this way. We'll meet back here in a few minutes. Don't let her leave."

"What's going on?" Bobbie asked.

"I'll tell you later," I said.

I ran up the street. I ducked into the dry cleaners. A flower shop. A coffee shop. Ran down an alleyway.

No Jules.

I met Bobbie back in front of the library. He hadn't found her either.

"What's happening?" Bobbie asked.

We walked over to the side of the library. I sat

on one of the stone benches. Will Shakespeare's, I think.

"She's in danger," I said. "I've got to find her."

I had to save her.

"I don't understand," Bobbie said. "Remember I'm just a poor dumb country boy."

I looked at him.

"I'm sorry," he said. "Not the time for humor."

"You know that bum we followed?" I asked. He nodded. "I didn't pick him randomly. I noticed something about him. He had this kind of glow, this dirty yellow glow around him. I wanted to find out what it meant, so I followed him."

"And it turned out you saved his life," Bobbie said. "Okay."

"Same with Sam," I said. "He had the same glow. And his mom and dad. The glow went away once they got in the taxicab to leave the house, once they were safe from Sam's dad. The bird had the yellow glow, too, until the next morning when it flew away."

"Do you see this glow all the time?" Bobbie asked.

I shook my head. "It comes and goes. I don't have any control over it. At least not as far as I can tell."

"All of these people—and the bird—were in

danger," Bobbie said. "Was that why they were glowing?"

"For whatever reason," I said, "I can tell when people are in danger of dying."

"Am I glowing?" Bobbie asked.

"No," I said.

"But Jules is?"

"Yes," I said.

"Then let's go find her."

We went to Pioneer Square and Forest Park. We didn't find her in either place. Of course, she could be almost anywhere in Forest Park. After all, it was 5,000 acres. The last place we looked was her apartment.

I knocked on the door. Bobbie stood behind me.

A man came to the door.

"Yeah, whaddya want?"

"Is Jules home?" I asked.

"Jules? Who the hell is Jules?" he asked.

I could see Typhoon Tina sitting at the table in the kitchen. She didn't look my way.

"Julie," I said. "I need to talk to Julie."

"She ain't here," he said. "She doesn't live here any more."

"Tina!" I called. "I need to find Jules. I think she's in trouble."

"You got that right," the man said. "She is trouble."

He slammed the door shut.

I didn't know where to go next. We stopped by Pythia Place and talked to Therese. She said Jules was too young for them to kick her out. They were legally responsible for her.

But she was gone anyway, and we didn't know where to find her.

"Tomorrow is our prom," Bobbie said to me as we walked away from Pythia Place. "She'll show up for that."

"That could be too late," I said.

"Hey, you said Sam was glowing from the time you met him," Bobbie said. "It wasn't until a couple of weeks later that he was actually in danger. Maybe it's the same for Jules."

And maybe it was all a coincidence. Maybe it was just something strange with my vision.

I wished that were true, but I knew it wasn't.

Bobbie had to go to work. I went back to our apartment. Mom was doing the dishes.

"How you doing, baby?" she asked.

She kept pretending everything was as it had been.

"Not good," I said. I sat at the table.

"I can't find Jules," I said, "and I think she's in trouble. I don't get it. I told her to come here if she needed anything. I just found out her mom or her mom's boyfriend kicked her out."

"I'm sure she'll be all right," Mom said. "She's

a survivor."

"No, she isn't," I said. "Haven't you looked
at her? She's all pretend. Trying to survive when
all the adults around her are assholes."

My mom didn't say anything for a moment. I
heard the water drain out of the sink.

"I guess you can relate," Mom said.

"Yeah, I can."

She came over and hugged me from behind.
I didn't shake her off or push away. It felt nice.
I sighed.

"It'll be all right," she said.

"I don't think it will be."

Thirteen

It was a long night. I dreamed I was on the floor playing with the blood puzzle. I heard screams. Then someone held her hand out to me. I looked up. It was Mom. She smiled. I took her hand.

Bobbie and I spent the day looking for Jules. We even wandered around the Blues Festival down by the water trying to find her. No luck. We stood outside the festival near the river and tried to figure out what to do next. People walked all around us. I saw a few glowing people. Marked people. I closed my eyes. I didn't want to see them. I couldn't help them. There were too many of them!

"Let's go to Forest Park and wait until she shows up," I said.

"If we don't come in our tuxes," Bobbie said,

"she will be so disappointed."

I looked at Bobbie. I wondered if he realized how serious this all was. What if Jules was dead right now. What if it was too late?

But we had tried to find her and couldn't. All we had left was the prom. She'd show up there. As long as she was all right, Jules would meet us at Forest Park for our prom.

"All right," I said. "Let's get home and get dressed."

We took the Max across the river and then we each hurried home. Bobbie said he'd get dressed and then we'd meet at my place.

The blue bomber wasn't in the parking lot. Mom must be at work. I was relieved. I didn't want to see her right now. I went inside. I put on the black tuxedo, and then I went into Mom's room to see how it looked in her full length mirror.

I didn't look half bad. Jules would be happy. Me bad in black, Bobbie pretty in pink.

I started to leave the room when I caught a glimpse of Mom's box, the one with the photograph of my father, on the closet shelf.

I went over to the closet and got the box. I opened it. Inside was a watch, money clip, a small silver comb, and two photographs. I took the photograph of my father out and put it in my shirt pocket. The other photograph was of a child.

He was smiling. Michael Dare, 3 1/2 years old.

Me. I stared at the boy's face.

He had no idea what catastrophe awaited him.

I put the photo back. I picked up the watch. It was a man's watch. It was still ticking. And a money clip. A silver comb. What were these things?

I heard the front door open and close.

"Baby?" Mom. "You home?"

In another moment, she was standing in the doorway.

"What are you doing with that?" she asked. She sounded angry. Surprised.

"I wanted the photo of my father," I said. "You said it was mine. What are these other things? Did you steal them?"

"One of my customers gave them to me," she said. She took the box from me and put it back up on the closet shelf. She pushed it to the back. "I was saving them to give them to you for your birthday."

"When is my birthday?" I asked. "My real birthday."

Mom stared at me. "Is it going to be like this forever?"

"I don't know, *Mom*," I said. "I just found out my real mother is dead. Give me a few minutes."

The doorbell rang.

I got up and left the room. I went to the front door and opened it. Bobbie stood on the threshold in his pink tuxedo.

"Please tell me I don't look like the Easter bunny," he said as he came inside.

"You don't look like the Easter bunny," I said.

Mom walked into the room. She looked at me and then at Bobby. She nodded.

"I like the boots," she said.

"Alley gator," Bobbie said.

"I'll be home late," I said.

I started to leave.

"Don't you have a hug for your dear old mom?"

I looked at Bobbie. He didn't say anything. I sighed. Then I walked over to Mom and hugged her. She put her arms around me and held me tightly.

"I love you," she whispered. "Everything I've ever done is because I love you."

Then she let me go.

Bobbie and I hurried away from the apartment building.

"You okay?" Bobbie asked.

"I'm above ground," I said.

It seemed to take forever to get to Forest Park. First the Max. Then the bus. Then we walked.

It was dusk. Twilight. The only light was from Bobbie's pink tuxedo. He was whistling. As we neared the park, the tall trees blocked out what little was left of daylight.

"Go on," Bobbie said. "Gotta tie my shoes."

I kept walking. I wanted to get to Jules, to make certain she was all right.

Suddenly the hair on my arms stood up. I shivered.

And I saw her.

The Shadow Woman.

No mistaking her this time.

She was just off the trailhead bent over something.

Someone.

Someone was sprawled on the ground. Someone wearing a shiny blue dress. Wasn't sure how I could see the color. But I could. Saw it because the person wearing it was glowing dirty yellow.

I knew it was Jules.

The Shadow Woman looked toward me. I could see her black eyes, like two coals burning in the twilight.

She was going to kill Jules.

Just like she had killed the homeless man in Phoenix.

Just like she had killed so many other people along the way.

I didn't hesitate. Not even for a second.

I raced toward her. I roared. "Get away from her!"

I ran. I was going to end this now once and for all.

I was going to save Jules.

She was still glowing. Still alive.

The Shadow Woman stepped aside before I could knock her down.

I almost lost my balance.

"I found her like this," the woman said. "She needs help."

"Get away from her!" I said again. "Jules! Jules! Can you hear me?"

I put my face close to hers. She was breathing. Still breathing.

I looked over at Bobbie.

"Call 911!" I yelled.

I reached my arms under Jules and I picked her up. "You'll be all right," I said. "You'll be all right."

I walked away from the park. I walked up the street, carrying Jules.

She couldn't die, couldn't die.

She lay limp in my arms.

"Keep breathing," I said.

I looked around. The Shadow Woman was gone.

One way or another, I was going to keep her from ever hurting anyone again.

The ambulance came quickly. They asked us if Jules was using any drugs. We told them we didn't know.

"Looks like fresh tracks," the EMT said. "She do black tar?"

He was asking us, Bobbie and me. We both shook our heads.

"She wouldn't use heroin," Bobbie said. "No."

"I don't really know," I said.

Jules looked so small on the stretcher, dressed in her shiny blue gown with sequins, all kinds of sequins, sequins that picked up the light from somewhere. She had sewn all of the sequins on the dress herself. It must have taken her forever.

They put her in the ambulance.

"We're going to Good Sam's if you want to follow," the EMT said.

"Is she going to be all right?" Bobbie asked.

"We'll see."

Then they were gone.

Bobbie picked up something from the ground. He held them up for me to see. One was a pair of pink wings, the other was a pair of black wings.

"It looks like you put them on using these shoulder straps," Bobbie said.

"They're huge," I said.

"She must have brought them for us to wear to the prom," Bobbie said.

"I wonder where hers are?" I said.

"These were all I found," he said.

We took the wings with us. I tucked the black ones under my arm, and we practically ran all the way to the hospital.

It seemed to take forever. Once we got there, a nurse asked us if we knew Jules's family. We told them we didn't know if they had a phone. Besides, her mother had kicked her out. They wanted an address anyway.

Finally the doctor came out and said Jules had overdosed. It was probably her first time using, and it had almost killed her. The doc thought Jules would be all right, but they had to wait and see. Her mother needed to be notified.

So drugs had almost killed her, not the Shadow Woman?

The doctor let us go see Jules.

She looked so pale.

She opened her eyes when we came into the room.

"Oh, don't you two look gorgeous," she said. She slurred her words.

"Yeah," Bobbie said. "But you look like shit."

"I think they cut my dress off," she said. "Can you find it for me?"

I took Jules's hand in mine. I leaned over and kissed it.

"Why didn't you come to my place?" I asked. "I would have taken care of you."

She closed her eyes. "Naw. Your mom said it would be better if I went someplace else."

"You came over?"

She nodded.

"Glad I met that lady," she said. "In the park. She helped me get to the trailhead. I was up in the woods. Felt so sick."

The lady? What lady?

"She was nice," Jules said.

"We better go tell her mom," Bobbie said.

"You go ahead," I said. "I need to do a couple of things."

Bobbie kissed Jules's forehead. Then we left the room and the hospital. I watched Bobbie run down the street to catch a bus. I had to walk a little. I had to do something. How could my mother have turned Jules away? How could she have done that?

Suddenly, the Shadow Woman stepped out of the shadow of the hospital. I moved away from her, but I didn't run. She didn't try to get any closer.

"What did you do to Jules?" I asked. "Why were you trying to hurt her?"

"I wasn't trying to hurt her," she said. "You know that. You know that things are not what they seem. The woman you know as your mother is not who you think she is."

"I know that!" I said. "She saved me after you killed my parents. We've been on the run all these years to get away from you. She tries to protect me from you. You're the one who wants to kill me! And why? I haven't done anything to you!"

"Haven't you ever wondered about your life?" she asked. "How strange it is. How everywhere you go, people die?"

"Of course people die," I said. "You're killing them."

She shook her head. "That's not what I do, Michael. Twelve years ago, you were going to die. You were sick. You were marked for death. She was supposed to help you die, but she didn't."

"What are you talking about?" I said.

"There are more things in this world than you will ever know," she said. "Than any of us will ever know. You've heard of the Angel of Death, haven't you? There isn't just one. There are many. They help the dying find their way to the next realm, the next incarnation. The woman you know as your mother didn't do what she was supposed to do. She took you instead."

"Are you saying my mother is the Angel of Death?" I started backing away. "This is crazy. You killed my parents and you would have killed me if I'd been there!"

"I didn't kill your parents," she said.

"Then who did?"

She looked at me.

"They will find her soon," the Shadow Woman said. "What she is doing isn't right. You found the clip and the watch."

I turned and started running.

I could barely breathe. Could hardly see.

What was happening?

Angel of Death?

The Grim Reaper?

I felt like I was going to throw up.

I took the Max and then the bus. I had to think. I had to find out. I had to do something. Be someone else.

I ran into our apartment. All the lights were on. Mom was packing.

"We've got to go," she said. "She's been here. I know it. I can feel it." She sounded frantic. My mother rarely sounded frantic.

My mother.

She wasn't my mother.

"You didn't tell me Jules was here," I said.

"I forgot," she said.

"She needed our help," I said.

"She had some lame story about her mother's boyfriend attacking her," Mom said. "She's all about the drama. We don't need any more drama. Get packing, baby. We got to get out of here!"

"Jules nearly died," I said. "She OD'd."

"See, I told you," Mom said. "She's trouble. We don't have to worry about her any more. We're outta here."

"I talked to her," I said. I followed my mom around the apartment, trying to get her attention.

"Jules? So she's all right."

"The Shadow Woman."

"You talked to her?"

"Is it true? Did you kill my parents?"

"What?" She hurried away from me and went into the bedroom, threw clothes into a suitcase. "Of course not."

"She says you're an Angel of Death," I said. "She said you were supposed to take me but you didn't."

Mom stopped and looked at me. Her eyes were black or hollow or terrified. "There isn't any such thing as an Angel of Death. That's ridiculous. That implies that someone is in charge and they send out their angels to help poor souls cross to the other side. It's not like that. There are all kinds of beings in this world and they get sustenance in different ways. Some creatures need air to survive. Others need to be in the water. Some kinds of bats feed off of the blood of other animals. You eat french fries and burgers. Some of us can see other realms, places, whatever you want to call them. We can point the way. We ask for a little coin in return, like Charon on the River Styx. People release so much energy when they die. We take that."

"You steal souls?"

"No," she said. "I don't even know if people have souls. It's just energy, baby. We get it and then we point them on their way. We know they're going to die because we can tell. Just like you can tell."

I felt like I was going to scream.

"You were sick," she said. "You were going to die. They were so stupid, your parents. You just needed a little medicine. I loved you as soon as I saw you. I had never felt that way about anyone. We're not supposed to interfere. That's a rule of our guild, our union, our little death club. There is a kind of balancing act in the Universe. I don't understand it. No one does. I took you, and yes, I killed your parents. I figured someone else had to go if you were staying. I thought that would make everything all right. Only it didn't. The others, the ones who do the kind of work I used to do, they've been after me all these years. They hold this death work sacred. We've all got to do something for a living, don't we? I kept taking people through the years. Sometimes I would see they were marked for death but they wouldn't die. So I hurried it along, that's all. I had to eat. I had to survive to take care of you. I made certain they all had peaceful journeys. And I hoped the exchange would keep the others away from us, would keep them from trying to take you."

"What others?" I asked. I rubbed my face. This was all too crazy. "That watch and money clip. That's from the man who died a couple of blocks from here, isn't it? You keep trophies?"

"I saved those things for you," she said. "Just like I said."

"You're a serial killer!" I said.

She took me by the shoulders. I had never realized how strong she was. I was suddenly terrified of her.

"You don't understand," she said. "It was all for the good. Look around. People worship death. They're all asking for it. You know they are! These parents who don't take care of their children, who drink and do drugs and abuse their kids. Look at the pollution. The diseases caused by the breakdown of the environment. The wars. All of it. They worship death! Otherwise they would fix it all, don't you think? I'm giving them what they want: Death. Come on, baby. I saved your life!"

"I'm not a baby!" I screamed. "This is so crazy! If I had died when I was supposed to, none of those other people would have died. They had families. They had children. They had lives! How could you do that to them?"

                                        Kim Antieau

"To save you," she said. "Aren't you listening?"

"But I was already saved!" I said.

She was crazy. She was the Angel of Death, and she was insane.

"Isn't there anything I can do to make you stop?"

She let go of my shoulders. "No, there isn't anything you can do. I will keep on protecting you until you're old and gray. And maybe even after that." She smiled. "You'll never have to worry about losing me."

I grabbed the car keys off the table and then I ran out of the apartment. I got into the blue bomber and drove away. I didn't know where I was going. I drove. And drove. After a while, I parked the car and started walking around.

I was supposed to be dead. Dead.

Did that make me one of the undead?

All this stuff about her being some kind of being like the Angel of Death, that couldn't be true, could it? This woman wanted a baby, wanted a child, so she killed my parents and kidnapped me. That was what had happened. Horrible, yes, but it didn't involve some kind of death club.

And the Shadow Woman. What was she? How did she figure into it?

It didn't matter if my mom was insane or if she was actually the Grim Reaper. People died because of me. They would continue to die.

I sat on the curb.

I couldn't do this any more. I had to stop her.

If I was gone, she wouldn't kill any more. Her reason—me—would be gone.

I knew what I had to do.

Fourteen

The sun was coming up. I got up off the curb and walked back to the car. I got in it and started it up. Hardly anyone else was out. I turned right off of 33rd and headed up the bottom part of the Fremont Bridge.

I knew how to stop my mother. Just like all those people on the Golden Gate Bridge. I had never had any control over my life. Ever. Not from the moment this woman who claimed to be my mother killed my parents and stole me away. I had lived with death every day for twelve years. No more. No more. I would free myself. I would free all those people she would kill if I stayed alive.

I would chose my own time, place, and method of death.

I was soon on the bridge. I pulled the car over

to the right side, parked it, turned it off, and got out. I walked over to the side of the bridge and looked out. The city was turning pink as the sun came up. I did like this place. I was sorry to leave it.

"Michael." I heard a whisper.

I turned around. The Shadow Woman stood a few yards away.

"I'm going to stop it," I said. "When I'm dead, she'll have no reason to keep killing. And you can go back to whatever you were doing before you started following us."

The woman shook her head.

"It isn't time for you to die," she said.

"It's twelve years past time," I said. I looked down. All I had to do was get over the three-foot railing and it would all be over.

"Death doesn't work that way," the woman said.

"You sound like my mother," I said. I tried to get up on the railing. "Or whoever she is. How did you always know where we were, by the way?"

"Michael."

This time it was Mom's voice.

How had she gotten here?

"Come with me," Mom said. "We'll start over. It'll be all right."

I thought of all the years I had spent with this woman. All the people who had been hurt. All the lies. The murders.

"I won't let you keep hurting people."

"And I won't let you jump," she said as she came toward me.

I leaned over slightly and put my hands on the railing. My body shook. I would never see seventeen. I would never kiss another girl. Never go to college. Never really live.

"If you stop me now, I'll kill myself some other way," I said. "You raised me. You know who I am, and you know I won't let you kill anyone else."

Mom stepped closer to me.

"Michael," she whispered. "Please come away from there."

I stared at her. She didn't look like a killer. A monster. She looked like my mother. She glanced over the railing.

"It's a long way down, baby," she said.

Then she lunged for me. Leapt at me. She was so quick. She always had been. I was quicker. Instinctively, I moved out of her way. The woman I had called Mom for twelve years lost her balance. Without a sound, she fell over the side of the bridge. I screamed as her body appeared to float for a second—maybe she had wings after all—and then she hit the roof of a building below, a building near the edge of the water. No sound. I watched her shatter into a million pieces, as though she was made of gray glass. Hundreds of crows flew down to her. Each picked up a piece of gray and carried it away.

I didn't understand. What had happened?

Could an angel of death die?

"Michael."

I turned around. The Shadow Woman was standing next to me.

I squinted at her. Saw her for the first time. I knew her. Hers was the face that looked down at me, sang to me, whispered to me, "My little angel."

It was her photograph I had seen in the *Oregonian*.

"You're Elizabeth Dare," I whispered.

"Used to be," she said.

"Mom," I said.

I put my arms around her. She embraced me. I could feel her. As though she was still alive. I could smell her.

"My little angel," she whispered.

Then we let each other go.

"It's all up to you now, Michael," she said. "It's your life."

"I can see when people are in trouble," I said. "When they're going to die. I don't know what to do. I can't help them all. I can't fix everyone, I can't make sure everyone is safe."

"I heard this story when I was a girl," Elizabeth said. "It was about a man who was walking on the beach. He saw another man picking up starfish and throwing them into the ocean. He asked the man what he was doing. 'The tide is going out and the sun is coming up and they will die unless they get back in the water.' The other man pointed out that the tide line went on for miles and miles. He could never get all the starfish back into the ocean. 'What you're doing is futile. You'll never make a difference.' The man picked up another starfish and threw it into the ocean. 'It made a different to that starfish.'"

"Is that your motherly way of saying I can't do everything, but I can do something?" I asked.

"You saved Sam," she said. "You saved that man who was drunk. You made a difference to them."

"Can you stay here with me?"

She smiled. "Be happy, my little angel."

I blinked.

And she was gone.

I didn't try to explain anything to anyone. I went to the apartment, got the box in Mom's room, and I threw all the contents away. I wiped away my prints, just in case.

Mom had paid the rent for the rest of the summer, so I figured I could stay there until I decided what to do next. I called her work and told them she had left town.

Bobbie and I went back to the Stone House in Forest Park. We found another set of wings. These ones were blue. We got dressed in our tuxes and we took all the wings to the hospital. We put ours on just before we went into the room.

Jules clapped.

"Yes, I knew you were angels all along!" she said. "What are those?" She was looking at the blue wings I was holding. "Did you make me some wings?"

"We thought you made them," Bobbie said. "So that we'd all have wings."

Jules shook her head. "No, I didn't. But they're beautiful. I'll keep them."

Jules came to stay with me while she got better. Tina threw out yet another boyfriend. She swore she was a changed woman. Jules said she'd wait and see what happened over the rest of the summer. Bobbie, Jules, and I liked hanging out at our apartment. We had our own kind of family. Some nights we went to the CloseUp. Some nights we watched movies at home.

When Jules was better, we did have our Stone House prom. We put on our wings, tuxes or dress. We danced and laughed.

We wondered who had left the wings.

I looked for the Shadow Woman in the shadows. It was hard to think of her as anything but the Shadow Woman. At least I wasn't afraid any more. At least not of shadows.

Some days I picked a marked person and I followed him or her. I tried to figure out how to keep them safe. Jules and Bobbie liked coming with me. Bobbie said we were like superheroes. The Angels of Life and Death he called us. He wasn't very good with titles. He finished the gay zombie comic. Joey and Harlan never got together, but Harlan and Jack did. He started a new comic series about the Angels of Life and Death. I tried to explain to him that wasn't how it worked. But I didn't understand enough to explain anything. Some days I missed the woman I had called Mom.

In August, Jules, Bobbie, and I borrowed bicycles and rode across the Fremont Bridge. Once a year they closed it to traffic and let bikes ride across. We were up above everything, it seemed. Floating. Flying. It felt great.

That night, Jules and Bobbie slept over. Jules in my bed, Bobbie on the couch. I sat on my mom's bed. The rent was coming due soon. I had to decide what to do. Should I go to my relatives and tell them who I was? Maybe one of them had a dog, a yard, a little yellow house. I had enough money to take the bus to someplace else. Back to Phoenix to visit Melissa? Or up to Seattle? Maybe go to Los Angeles after all.

I took a coin out of my pocket.

Maybe I could get Jules and Bobbie to come with me.

Heads or tails?

I tossed the coin up into the air.

And caught it.

About the author

Kim Antieau lives with her husband in the Pacific Northwest, near Portland, Oregon, in a county where Bigfoot is a protected species.